The YOGA MAMAS

The YOGA MAMAS

Katherine Stewart

BERKLEY BOOKS, NEW YORK

THE BERKLEY PUBLISHING GROUP
Published by the Penguin Group
Penguin Group (USA) Inc.
375 Hudson Street, New York, New York 10014, USA
Penguin Group (Canada), 10 Alcorn Avenue, Toronto, Ontario M4V 3B2, Canada
(a division of Pearson Penguin Canada Inc.)
Penguin Books Ltd., 80 Strand, London WC2R 0RL, England
Penguin Group Ireland, 25 St. Stephen's Green, Dublin 2, Ireland (a division of Penguin Books Ltd.)
Penguin Group (Australia), 250 Camberwell Road, Camberwell, Victoria 3124, Australia
(a division of Pearson Australia Group Pty. Ltd.)
Penguin Books India Pvt. Ltd., 11 Community Centre, Panchsheel Park, New Delhi—110 017, India
Penguin Group (NZ), Cnr. Airborne and Rosedale Roads, Albany, Auckland 1310, New Zealand
(a division of Pearson New Zealand Ltd.)
Penguin Books (South Africa) (Pty.) Ltd., 24 Sturdee Avenue, Rosebank, Johannesburg 2196, South Africa

Penguin Books Ltd., Registered Offices: 80 Strand, London WC2R 0RL, England

This book is an original publication of The Berkley Publishing Group.

This is a work of fiction. Names, characters, places, and incidents either are the product of the author's imagination or are used fictitiously, and any resemblance to actual persons, living or dead, business establishments, events, or locales is entirely coincidental.

PRINTING HISTORY
Berkley trade paperback edition / July 2005

Library of Congress Cataloging-in-Publication Data

Stewart, Katherine Silberger.
    The yoga mamas : a novel / Katherine Silberger Stewart.—1st ed.
        p. cm.
    ISBN 0-425-20263-1
        1. Yoga—Fiction. 2. Pregnant women—Fiction. 3. Female friendship—Fiction. I. Title.

PS3619.T4944Y64 2005
813'.6—dc22
                                                                                        2004055414

PRINTED IN THE UNITED STATES OF AMERICA

10 9 8 7 6 5 4 3 2 1

For Matthew and Sophia

The author wishes to thank Alison McCabe, editor; Andrew Stuart, agent; Rae Silberger, mother; and Mim Udovitch, angel.

The YOGA MAMAS

1

Once you start the journey, there is no return.

—CHRISTY TURLINGTON, *LIVING YOGA: CREATING A LIFE PRACTICE*

"Om shanti, shanti, shanti."

A dozen pregnant women and I sit cross-legged on the floor and chant in unison. After two months of prenatal yoga, I still don't know what the chants mean. I don't want to know. When your belly is the size of a vending machine, it just feels good to be surrounded by other equally large women.

"Loka namasta, suki no babantu."

Years ago, I thought of pregnancy as a fashion statement. I pictured myself flaunting my new shape in luscious, form-fitting silk, my hands resting on a teacup-sized belly. I guess I was planning to have a celebrity pregnancy, the kind you read about in style magazines.

I was clueless.

Richard and I planned this pregnancy. Or at least the part you think you can plan. Then baby turned into a living nugget inhabiting my body, and the whole thing seemed to spin out of control. I ordered a shelf full of books about childbirth but might as well have bought horror videos. Miscarriages, toxic reactions, prenatal depression, postnatal depression—there were just too many ways the whole thing could go horribly wrong. Friends and relatives happily volunteered bloodcurdling stories, like the one about a friend of a friend whose labor lasted three days and nights, and so-and-so "whose coochie was never the same."

"Shanti, shanti, shanti."

Hasharama is located in the glossy heart of Soho. Bona fide celebrities sometimes show up in class, and Prada-clad students browse for herbal body oils, Tibetan rugs, and overpriced meditation videos in the gift shop. Portraits of spiritual overachievers stare down benignly from the walls: Deepak Chopra, various bearded gurus, Gwyneth Paltrow. For a place devoted to "spiritual liberation," it has a distinctly authoritarian streak. Written exhortations governing almost every aspect of client behavior are taped to all the walls.

SAVE A TREE: USE THE AIR DRYER. OM SHANTI.
SAVE THE OCEANS: USE WATER SPARINGLY. OM SHANTI.
ATTEND TO YOUR BELONGINGS!
MANAGEMENT NOT LIABLE. OM SHANTI.

Our instructor's name is Gaia, and she wears her gray hair in a long braid. "Your body exists in the past, and your spirit exists in the future," she says. Gaia's idea of yoga, like the amber earrings dangling over her sinewy shoulders, is very 1970s.

"Once you begin the journey, there is no return," she intones.

Life as I have always known it is definitely over. I squeeze my bloated feet in my hands, amazed to discover they are even puffier today. I scan my internal body monitors. *Back pain? Check. Leg cramps? Check.* My body is acting like it has a mind of its own—a wanton, reckless mind with no respect for earlier ideas of self. "You know, I'm *pregnant*," I say to Richard, often. "I know," he responds, like we're talking about the weather. "Five months now."

"I don't *really* have fat feet," I mutter to myself.

"Rise! Inhale!" Gaia barks.

I roll up onto my feet. Gaia lifts her head majestically, closes her eyes, and spreads her arms wide. The rest of us follow her in the Sun Salutation. As I close my eyes, I feel my baby flutter. I think about the distant future. I picture my teenage daughter and me walking through a sunny field of wildflowers. "Mom, you're the best," my daughter is saying. Then I notice she has triple-pierced her tongue.

"Exhale into Downward Dog!"

I always figured that when I got pregnant we'd move to the countryside—where the whole family might blossom among the sunny neighbors and wild daisies. Instead, we are staying in Manhattan, because, as Richard said in one infamous argument, "it's *the* power center in seventeenth-century Dutch studies."

I let out my breath and reach down to the floor. I move one

foot back, then the other, allowing my belly to hang suspended like a wrecking ball between splayed hands and feet. To either side of me, a dozen very large women are posed identically, hands on the floor, rear ends pointing skyward.

"Move into Viparita Karani," orders Gaia. *The Legs Up the Wall pose.*

I roll my body close to the wall and raise my legs. The effects of reverse gravity make me feel giddy. From this angle, I spot a few dark hairs sprouting from the knuckle of my big toe. I glance at the line of raised feet to either side of me. The pedicures are impeccable. By comparison, my unvarnished toes look bestial.

The regulars at Hasharama are women who live in Soho's two-million-dollar loft apartments. They eat twenty-dollar gourmet sandwiches and can afford to spend two hours every day in the middle of the day at yoga class. They sport perfect blowouts and heavy rocks—diamond solitaires the size of cocktail nuts, or dazzling, multicolored rings from Cartier and Reinstein/Ross. They look like the silky extras from a Jaguar commercial, whereas *I* am more the Rent-a-Wreck type. I live on the northern side of Houston Street in a forlorn stack of concrete blocks that houses university staff. The rents are insultingly low compared to the local market, which puts them in the "barely affordable" category for Richard and me. My participation in Hasharama's exclusive yoga program comes courtesy of the university's enlightened insurance policies; my presence in the middle of every working day is one of the perks of being an unmotivated freelancer.

"Inhale. Escort your breath out of your body. Now open into Warrior One!"

Gaia narrows her eyes into an appropriately martial expression as we all spread our feet wide, right knees bent, and clutch imaginary swords over our heads, trying to lower our bodies close to the ground without tumbling. Out of the corner of my eye, I watch Susan. As always, she moves reverently from one perfectly executed posture into another. She has long, honey-blond hair and a lean body, on which her enormous belly bobs like a balloon on a stick. Her eyes seem distant, ethereal, perhaps a little fragile. A silver chain with a pair of small seashells hangs from her neck. Everybody knows she is Gaia's favorite pupil.

I think of her as the girl with the vitamin fetish.

Before class she downs several different pills of various sizes and colors. One day I asked her about it. "I have this amazing nutritional therapist," she replied. "She knows exactly how to balance my *chi*."

To my other side, I can see a petite, businesslike woman with green eyes, a shock of carrot-red hair, and a large, teardrop-shaped beauty mark riding on her upper lip. Her belly is so big it seems she's renting it from someone else.

Next to her is a designer blond, the kind of woman who won't wear anything that doesn't have a label prominently displayed. When she finds one of the positions uncomfortable, which happens frequently, she sighs dramatically and wilts into a tangled lump on her Marc Jacobs yoga mat.

Dominating the center of the room is an olive-toned six-footer. She is unmistakably Spanish. From her supernatural bone structure, I've decided she is a model. I have to consciously avert my gaze from her so as not to be caught staring.

Truth be told, I find the Hasharama ladies a little scary. I do look forward to seeing them, if only to compare bellies silently. But I can't picture any of them eating cold take-out from the carton night after night. They aren't people like *me*. Richard thinks it's all a big joke. "Maybe you have more in common than you think," he said, when I told him about the Hasharama regulars. "Even the rich get pregnant."

Suddenly one of the women lets out an exasperated snort. *"Eeaaooouu!"*

It is the New Girl. She is an immense, gangly woman and she wears her pregnancy like a basketball strapped to her waist. She has big, brown, because-I'm-worth-it hair and a permanently startled expression on her face, as though surprised to find herself alive, pregnant, and in a prenatal yoga class.

"Oh my god, that bagel is sitting right in the middle of my stomach like a *log,*" she says to no one in particular, her voice screeching in from the wrong side of the Brooklyn-Queens Expressway.

Gaia inhales noisily, implicitly chastising the New Girl for her outburst.

"I am *so* stiff!!" the New Girl continues.

Hasharama has an unstated code of silence. No one has dared interrupt the flow of karmic energy by speaking during a class before. But the New Girl seems oblivious to yoga studio etiquette.

"I used to be able to get a *Mack truck* through my legs. Now look at me!"

Women are tilting their Warrior Ones in her direction. One or two sly smirks break out. Gaia shoots the New Girl a warning look, then closes her eyes, to draw our focus back and inward.

"*Every*body, now. Lift up your arms, reach for the sky," she instructs in a voice laden with spiritual responsibilities.

New Girl punctures Gaia's spiritual aura with a nasal groan. "Aaawwww!"

"Moving on to Lion's Breath. Inhale!" Gaia snaps.

Sitting on my knees, toes tucked under me, I extend my tongue out as far as it will go, roll my eyes back into my head, and tighten every muscle in my face. Then I hiss noisily.

"Hey, uh, excuse me?"

Gaia looks up with dismay. "Can you explain exactly how this is supposed to help my baby?" the New Girl asks. " 'Cause, right now, it's making me feel like a nut job!" She looks around the room and giggles. Even her giggle sounds like Queens Boulevard.

Our Lion's Breath expressions dissolve into laughter as the rest of us giggle back.

"I feel like a nut job these days too!" says the petite redhead. "After work, all I do is sleep and eat, sleep and eat."

"I *wish* that I could sleep," chimes in the Spanish model. "Every time I lie down, my baby starts to kick me. Boom, boom, boom! I am going to have a party girl on my hands!"

"This one always wakes up during yoga class," says Susan, the vitamin-popper. "I feel him moving now. I bet he'll come out doing Downward Dog!"

I hear myself adding, "I hope mine doesn't come out doing Lion's Breath!"

We all laugh some more. Suddenly it is our class, and we take it over. We twitter merrily, comparing bellies and mocking our pregnancy symptoms, until Gaia sighs and shakes her head, as though resigning herself to the cruel fact that the sacred knowledge of the ancients is wasted on twenty-first-century philistines.

After class, we roll up our yoga mats and head back for the changing room. The designer blond and a few other, less pregnant women scurry off. The rest of us linger, waiting to see what will come of our newfound camaraderie. Susan pops two yellow pills, then tries wrapping her Balinese sarong in a dozen different ways. I loiter indecisively. Then the New Girl goes to work.

She pours herself into skintight jeans that leave her tumescent belly exposed and rolls over to the Spanish model, who is sliding into a flounced red skirt and tight black tank top that reveals every inch of her tan-colored midriff. Although I have been walking around town in the kind of extra-large T-shirts that leave people guessing whether I am pregnant or just dieting unsuccessfully, I find myself thinking, *why not?*

"I'm Gigi!" New Girl whispers loudly, grabbing her classmate's arm conspiratorially. "Let's go to lunch!"

The Spanish model smiles in agreement and introduces herself as "Isla."

Then Gigi rolls over to Susan and picks up her hand.

"How do you do?" Susan says, as if it's a peculiar kind of handshake.

"That ring is *beyond!*" Gigi shrieks. She holds it up to the light, admiring the stone—a large, square-cut sapphire set in finely worked platinum. I notice that Gigi herself is hefting a forklift-grade diamond.

"Thanks," says Susan. "It's been in the family—my husband's family—a long time."

Susan is definitely in on the lunch.

A cell-phone ring cuts through the room. The petite redhead fishes her phone out of a black Birkin bag and flips it open. "Yeah, this is Margaret. Who else do you think is going to answer my phone? . . . No, I did not tell that *insect* that the brief was complete. Subsection 2-A-3 is bullshit. . . ."

A corporate lawyer, I conclude.

Gigi shouts at her, "We're going to lunch!" and Margaret's mouth drops open in amazement at the interruption. Then, after a pause, she says, "OK," and gets rid of her call.

I am sure I have not made the cut. I curse my Old Navy sweats and start to leave.

"Hey, Laura, where ya goin'?"

I turn around, stunned. She learned my name? Gigi was looking at me, seeming almost hurt. "Ain't you comin', hon?"

That was the beginning of my yoga mama summer.

2

Yoga exists in the world because everything is linked.

—DESIKACHAR

Gigi led the way to the restaurant with her belly. At her side, Isla, too, thrust her bare midsection defiantly out to the front, as if daring anyone to comment. Susan, Margaret, and I followed behind them, and the sidewalks opened up before us like the parting of the Red Sea. Five pregnant women in Soho are an arresting sight. People scuttled out of our way. Across the street they stopped to look. We were loud, large, and in charge.

A good-looking guy snagged his eyes on Isla's winsome face and panned the rest of ours. Then he did a double take on our bellies, and his come-hither look suddenly changed to one of panic. "Don't worry, sweetheart, none of them is yours," Gigi said as we sashayed past. We laughed, and I felt a surge of power. With my new, supersized pals, I no longer viewed the streets as an obstacle course of aggressive shoppers and dog walkers. *Soho is ours,* I thought with glee, as we approached the corner of West Broadway and Prince and burst through the doors of the Healthy Harvest.

The Healthy Harvest is the kind of restaurant that specializes in ingredients collected by indigenous peoples in remote locations during limited growing seasons. When our group of five appeared at the entrance, the fashionably undernourished patrons turned toward us with a kind of morbid fascination. Isla especially drew stares. The background commotion quieted and heads moved in unison as she picked her way through the tables, her red skirt swishing behind her. Even had she worn my old sweats, I thought, her otherworldly beauty would have shone through. But Isla seemed utterly indifferent to the drama of her physical presence. When we arrived at our table, Gigi frowned at the cramped arrangements. "Cupcake, do you mind?" she shouted across the room to our waitress. Without waiting for an answer, she pushed two tables together and cleared away the surrounding chairs.

We sat down and studied the menu intensively. Pregnancy involves a serious change in one's relationship to food. My salad days were definitely over; I'd been eating like a construction worker—a construction worker with bizarre cravings and aversions. In short, I had become every waiter's nightmare. "I'll have the Himalayan soufflé—but no mushrooms. Did you get that? *No mushrooms,*" Gigi said. "I haven't been able to look at a mushroom for months," Margaret agreed. I asked for the Free-Range Tofu without green beans, and Susan sheepishly volunteered to eat my beans for me. Isla went on so long about how she wanted her emu steak cooked we all began to giggle. After the disconcerted waitress left with our orders, Susan said to no one in particular, "Gaia is so inspiring!"

"Yeah," Gigi said skeptically, "don't get me wrong, sweet pea, I love Gaia. But I don't go for all that granola crap. And I'm waiting for the day she trips over those earrings! Speaking of which . . ." She reached over and gently tapped the two shells dangling from Susan's necklace.

Susan blushed and smiled. "Oh, this? This is something my husband and I . . ."

"Tell us the story, sugar," Gigi said. "When I see a couple of clams on a girl's neck, I know it's gotta be a good one!"

She was wandering along the edge of the ocean in East Hampton, Susan said, a shy, twenty-something graduate of Miss Porter's School for Girls and part-time schoolteacher. She was so absorbed in the discovery of a perfectly formed miniature clamshell that she didn't notice a handsome man with curly black hair standing in front of her. When she looked up, he offered her the most exquisite shell: a tiny, marbled conch. His name was Harcourt, and he had deep blue eyes. His parents lived on an oceanfront estate nearby, and he was visiting for the weekend. He lived and worked in the city.

"Oh, does your husband work in finance?" Gigi cut her off. "So does mine!"

She said it as though both of them were members of an exclusive club. *The Trophy Wives Club,* the brat in me thought.

"My Milton is old Boston," Gigi was saying. "He's a real Brahmin."

In her mouth, "Brahmin" sounded like "Bra Man," and I could see a frown of incomprehension cross Isla's brow.

"We're talking a stateroom suite on the *Mayflower,*" Gigi said. "He's the real deal."

Susan nodded, slightly embarrassed, unsure if she should continue.

"It ain't easy breaking the ice with these Pilgrim people," Gigi kept talking. "But my Milton is on my side. He may seem like a softie, but inside he's rock solid. When we met, I was busting my ass working as a party planner. He said, 'You quit your job 'cause I'm taking care of you now!' We're like this——" She clenched her fist. Then she gave Susan a penetrating look. "So tell us the rest of the story!"

Susan picked up where she had left off, with her Prince Charming on the beach holding out his exquisite seashell. Harcourt invited her to an organic juice bar close by. They talked about the beauty of the ocean, about the infinite variety of seashells, and the mysteries of evolution. Within a year they were married.

"And here's the conch, and here's the clamshell," Susan said proudly, as she held out the pendant for us to inspect. The two miniature crustaceans had been carefully shellacked and held in place on a platinum mount.

Susan lives in an enchanted storybook, I thought, *a gilded collection of fairy tales about her life she writes in her mind*. She had the kind of expensive incompetence that usually makes me want to bonk people over the head.

Gigi turned to Isla. "How about you? How long have you been with your husband?"

"I am not married," said Isla flatly.

"Sweetie, I'm sorry."

"No, it is not sorry," Isla said simply. "Antonio and I, we are together for almost seven years." She shrugged. "Anyway, he is married to his restaurants."

Antonio owned a string of trendy eateries. His latest project, Isla told us, was Extra Virgin, a soon-to-be-opened restaurant specializing in dishes prepared with premium oils from around the world. There was going to be a tasting bar at which one could sample the first cold press from the groves of Andalusia, Tuscany, Tunisia.

"Sounds like a place I could take my out-of-town clients," said Margaret.

"Antonio doesn't care about the business people." Isla tossed her head with annoyance. "He wants his Extra Virgin to be place for the single people to meet each other. He says it will be 'the filet-mignon section of the meat market.' He is sending free passes to all of the modeling agencies, so that his restaurant will be filled up with pretty young girls. He even has made an erotic oil to sell at the restaurant. It is called the Extra Virgin Sauce. He thinks that the men and women will like to pour it on each other." She wrinkled her nose with distaste.

It sounded silly to me too. But Gigi looked excited.

"Your Antonio must be a real sex fiend!"

"I wish that he could be a sex fiend with me. He will not touch me since when I have become pregnant. He is afraid to hurt the baby." Isla rolled her eyes. "We have not made sex in so long, I forget how this baby has happened."

Secretly, I felt relieved to discover that Isla's sex life left something to be desired. It made her seem less like the member of a genetically modified race of supermodels, and more like an ordinary woman facing some of the usual problems with guys.

"Anyway, I never see him now," Isla continued. "Either he is working or he is at the gym. He says he wants to have the right image for his restaurant. He has to fit into his leather pants for the opening night." She twirled her finger around her temple in the sign for loco. "We are going to have a baby, and all he can think about is fitting into his leather pants."

"I think men don't really understand the concept of pregnancy," I sighed.

I started cataloging some of Richard's most obvious faults, beginning with the fact that my husband of two years thought of pregnancy as some sort of abstract condition, like membership in a book club. "For the first few months I couldn't sleep," I said. "I'd just lie in bed all night, worrying about how our lives are going to change. Richard would wake up after a good night's sleep and say, 'Worrying is not an efficient use of your time. All the books say so.'" Efficiency is Richard's favorite word. I kept telling him pregnancy is not efficient! "Besides," I added, "we can't agree on a name. So far he only likes two."

"What are they?" Susan asked.

"Hannah and Anna," I replied.

"Classy," Gigi drawled approvingly. "Classy and, like, proper."

"But I think those names are a bit boring, don't you think so?" Isla chimed in.

"That's what *I* keep saying." I nodded.

As we unraveled the characters of the fathers of our children over our special-order dishes, I found myself feeling more relaxed than I had since I'd discovered my pregnancy. My usual friends weren't any more clued in than Richard. Few of them were in steady relationships, let alone married, and none had had kids. They'd been treating me like I had some sort of unfortunate medical affliction.

"I can't believe you think you're ready to have a baby," said my hard-partying public relations friend. I wanted to say to her, "I'm thirty-three years old; how much more 'ready' am I supposed to be?" At least my yoga mamas understood. "I know!" we exclaimed over and over again as we saw how much we had in common. Being pregnant together was so much more fun than being pregnant alone.

Only Margaret looked a little uneasy. Margaret was the only one of us holding down a daily job—not counting my imaginary freelance career and Isla's occasional modeling assignments. She was a partner at a prestigious downtown corporate law firm— Cadwaspy & Preppier, or something like that—and at her doctor's recommendation she had come to an arrangement where she would work only afternoons through her last four months of pregnancy. She was also a single mother, and all the talk about men seemed to be making her uncomfortable. Since she seemed pretty straightforward, I asked her point-blank what happened to the father of her child.

His name was Jonathan, and he had once been a junior partner at Cadwaspy. "I'm at the office sixteen hours a day; who else am I going to date?" she said. After years of working side by side, she explained, they started flirting over legal briefs. Then one evening they decided to go to a late-night movie. During the movie, he kissed her. "It felt like high school." She smiled ruefully. "Since we worked together, it was completely illegal. It was totally hot."

A couple of days later, after working together on a case long after closing time, they left the office together in search of late-night sushi. On the way back, thirsty from all the soy sauce, they decided to stop in at a grocery store to buy a couple of bottles of beer. It was a desolate downtown branch of the Gristedes chain.

"I don't know, I just really wanted him," she said dryly. "We were in the dairy aisle. No one was looking. I grabbed his shirt and pulled him toward me. He started kissing me and feeling me up. So I attacked him. I yanked down his pants and pulled his—"

By now, Margaret had everybody's attention. "I mean, I'm thirty-nine years old," she said defensively. "I haven't got time to mess around!"

Gigi demanded more details.

"I guess you could say that Jonathan was holding me up in the whipping cream section, directly facing the security camera." Margaret pursed her lips and smiled. "Jonathan is pretty . . . strong."

Our table burst into giggles and hoots. Patrons at one or two neighboring tables widened their eyes.

"It would have been fine if I hadn't decided to buy the beer. I didn't have cash, so I paid with a credit card," Margaret deadpanned. "A couple of days later my bosses got a call from Gristedes. The whole scene was on videotape, the guy said, and there was no need for forensic analysis to determine the identities of the suspects: They had the details on my credit card."

This was not the sort of thing that *happened* at Cadwaspy & Co. "I mean, most of my colleagues think you order babies out of a J. Crew catalog."

Because there was a corporate policy against "intramural" relationships, either Jonathan or Margaret had to go. "My boss never got along with Jonathan," Margaret said. "This gave him a perfect excuse."

So Jonathan lost his job. He left without saying good-bye.

When she later found out she was pregnant, Margaret left a message on Jonathan's voice mail. "Hi, it's Margaret. There's something important I need to tell you. Please call me ASAP." He left a message in return, saying, "You've done enough damage. So fuck off. And I'm not shopping at Gristedes anymore."

Margaret called twice more, trying to reach him, but he ignored her.

"Bastard!" Gigi exclaimed.

"You are sure that he is the father?" Isla asked.

"Yeah, I'm sure. Unfortunately for him, that was the only time I've had sex in the past two years. Anyway, a DNA test will eventually confirm it."

"Is it possible he doesn't even know you're—" I started to ask.

"He'll find out when the time is right," Margaret cut in, with quiet determination. A fierce look crossed her face and I pictured her enemies volunteering to eat poisoned sushi rather than face this woman in court.

"Well, honey, you've got balls," Gigi announced, "to do this on your own."

"You know what? Fuck Jonathan. We're gonna be fine," Margaret answered resolutely. "I love my boy already."

Across from me, Susan was nervously fingering the seashells on her necklace. I wondered if Margaret's tough talk had offended her. "In a way you're lucky it was so easy," she said, rubbing her belly gently. "It took me a lot of help to get this little one."

"Sweetheart," Gigi said. "Did you have to . . ."

"I . . . we haven't told anyone," Susan said quietly, making a gesture of frustration. "But honestly, it's been so hard I don't think I'll believe he's real until he arrives. I wish it could have been as easy as picking up a quart of milk."

I had always blithely told myself that if I couldn't conceive a child, I'd go on with life as usual, and maybe adopt eventually. But seeing the look of anxiety on Susan's face, I felt incredibly lucky to be pregnant. I gave my little girl a thankful squeeze through my belly, and she hiccoughed in reply.

Susan gathered all our sympathetic looks together in her gentle smile. "I feel that we are all connected with each other," she said. "We're here for a reason. Everything is linked."

My winter of baggy sweatshirts gave way to a glorious summer of low-slung skirts and T-shirts. In the balmy days of June and July, I even tied colorful sarongs around my hips and thrust my naked belly out right alongside Gigi and Isla. "Wow!" said a neighbor skeptically, when she passed me in the hall one day. "I guess pregnant women are letting it all hang out these days."

"Guess so." I *hmmm*-ed, thrusting out my belly even further.

Richard said, "Maybe the rich really *are* different."

3

Remember, yoga practice is like an obstacle course—
many obstructions are put in the way for us
to pass through.

—SWAMI SATCHIDANANDA

In the afternoons, after yoga class and lunch, I would some-
times waddle over to Gigi's apartment on Sullivan Street. While
we yoga mamas were forming our own little tribe, it was Gigi
who was my true partner. In some ways, we couldn't have been
more dissimilar: She had a rule ready for every situation, whereas
my universe seemed to be totally ad hoc. But I was drawn to her
self-confidence. She was all brass.

We liked to while away the daylight hours at her place, snack-
ing our way through the take-out menus of Lower Manhattan
and watching daytime TV. She and Milton lived in a huge

three-bedroom apartment along with about six bedrooms' worth of furniture. The décor looked like it had been airlifted in from Darien, Connecticut. Elaborate walnut cabinets fought with dark-green-plaid sofas for floor space, and silver-framed photographs of innumerable friends and ancestors jostled over the fireplace and on every available surface. At the far end of the living room, there was a small oasis of order, a desk with neatly arranged papers and pens lined up parallel to the edges and a framed certificate of graduation from Amherst College overhead.

"That's Milton's corner," Gigi explained one lazy afternoon as I picked my way through the obstacle course in her living room and plopped down on an overstuffed armchair. Gigi turned the central air-conditioning unit to maximum, then threw herself on the sofa. She found the remote underneath some well-thumbed magazines and flicked on one of the daytime talk shows. With the steady, soothing patter of a live studio audience in the background, I slipped off a pair of ballet flats that I'd picked up at a Sigerson Morrison sample sale and stretched my legs, trying to head off some mild cramping in my calf muscle.

Before, I never fully appreciated the virtues of daytime TV. I thought of afternoon programming as discount-store chocolates, the kind that leave you feeling ashamed and slightly nauseous. But pregnancy involves a serious change in viewing habits and interests. Now I found that I couldn't watch anything that involved bloodshed or heavy machinery—which ruled out most of Hollywood, not to mention the evening news. Documentaries about rescued kittens, on the other hand, were suddenly—inexplicably—highly appealing. At Gigi's house, we loved the talk shows best of all.

Plus, I told myself, I *had* to watch more television, because that was part of my job. As a marketing consultant, I needed to keep up with trends in advertising. At least, that was the excuse I gave to Gigi. It would have been more convincing if I actually had some paying clients. Freelance consulting was supposed to be the perfect way to continue my career in advertising while having a baby. I didn't have much of a choice in the matter; shortly after I'd told my boss, Robin, about my pregnancy, she announced the agency was downsizing. "Don't worry honey," she told me, handing me my severance check. "If you consult for us, you'll make just as much money as before. And you can work from home in your pajamas!"

My first assignment as a freelancer was to propose a campaign for Amalgamated Motor's brand new Cheetah Convertible. With a twelve-cylinder engine, the highest power-to-weight ratio of any car on the road, and a streamlined body modeled on the stealth fighter jet, the Cheetah had no room to spare for a backseat or a trunk. Its two tons of "untamed energy" were intended for the driver and a single lucky passenger.

"It's a getaway car for fat, balding men," Robin chirped.

It was my idea of an utterly useless machine.

The campaign for the Cheetah had left me stumped until one day in yoga class I found inspiration. While we were doing our Sun Salutations, Gaia launched into one of her hypnotic chants: "Free yourself from worry. Exist in the moment. Lose the baggage of the material world."

Lose the baggage, I thought—the perfect slogan for the trunkless, backseat-less Cheetah! I sketched out a whole campaign based on the theme. I drew up a storyboard for a television ad: A haggard-looking woman (possibly pregnant) presents a handsome young man (presumed to be her husband) with an enormous pile of luggage (his family's); he looks at the camera in distress; he walks past a clunky SUV, hops into the Cheetah, and zooms off in a cloud of dust. Voice-over says: Lose the baggage. I wrote up a mock radio ad: "They say you can't take it with you . . . we say, lose the baggage." I express-mailed the proposal to Robin.

That was over two months ago.

Her assistants always offered some friendly excuse about how she was out of town, in a meeting, getting around to it, or whatever, but somehow she hadn't gotten around to returning my calls. At this point, I figured my Lose the Baggage proposal was the favorite topic of office jokes. "Guess what Fat Foot sent in," I pictured them smirking by the watercooler. "She wants to pitch a car to deadbeat dads! First she gets pregnant, then she loses her mind!" Gigi thoughtfully poked me every time a car ad came on, but for the first time in my professional life, I found myself far more interested in Dr. Phil than in commercials.

"All that fighting?" Gigi said, on another one of our lazy afternoons. "That's like my family at the dinner table. Remember that show about priests with secret wives and kids stashed away somewhere?"

I nodded.

"I tried to get my brother on it," she said, wide-eyed. "The show's producers said he'd be *perfect*. But then he went into rehab."

Gigi's mother and sister weren't any less colorful than her

defrocked, ex-drunk brother. The mother had a thing for young men—"like, really young," Gigi would say—and her sister spent her time in and out of various religious cults. But the worst was her father. He had been a professional gambler, smoked two packs a day, married three times, and died before he was sixty. "When the numbers came up right, things were great," said Gigi. "When he was down, everything tanked. One day he finally bet the house. And I do mean the house. We ended up on the street. They pulled me out of school because they couldn't afford the fees. Then, like, things got weird."

I let her stories wash over me without allowing any of the details to stick. I knew what it was like to lose a father. Sometimes it hurt too much to be reminded.

"Me, I'm the *normal* one!" she said, matter-of-factly, more than once, when she was wrapping up a tale of her family's dirty laundry. She had a certain it-can't-be-true look she used to punctuate her stories, a look of complicit disbelief, like you had both just witnessed a dog open its mouth and start reciting the Constitution. She threw me that look now. "I'm a fifties housewife. Plain vanilla. I just want to take care of my Milton and stay home with the baby."

Gigi was the kind of woman I used to think of as a "streetwalker"—the kind who wore diamond studs and Cartier tank watches, who regarded the term "high maintenance" as a compliment, and who wouldn't think of dating a guy unless he worked on Wall Street. But the more Gigi and I talked, the more I began to imagine myself with one of these men. They sent flowers. They took you on ski trips. Gigi had been reticent about how she met Milton. After we'd been sharing Dr. Phil for a few weeks, I got up the courage to press her on the subject.

"I was dating a lot of different guys," she started. "I just couldn't make up my mind. Then I met my Milton, and I realized he was different. Like, he's *not* the kind of guy you'll walk in on screwing some other broad on the kitchen table." On their second date, Milton gave Gigi a diamond heart pendant from Tiffany. "He said, 'This is for the girl who stole my heart.' " She held it up for me, and it sparkled in the late-afternoon sunlight. She and Milton dated for six weeks. Then, on a wild weekend in the Bahamas, he proposed. They got married three weeks later. I couldn't help but remember Richard's lackluster proposal to me. "I suppose we should consider marriage now" were his exact words. Hearing about Gigi's whirlwind romance made me wish we weren't such a sensible pair, and I said as much.

"You don't know how lucky you are, sugar pie," Gigi said. She stared at me for a long time, long enough to make me feel a little uncomfortable. "OK," she said, exhaling noisily. "I'm gonna tell you, but you have to promise you won't tell anyone. Promise!"

I promised.

"Do you swear on your mother's grave?" she asked.

In fact, my mom was alive and well in San Diego, but this seemed serious. "I swear," I said.

"I trust you," she said. "I mean, you know I love all the girls. But, like, on a personal level, you're the one I can turn to."

I almost swooned with flattery.

She picked up my left hand. " 'Cause you ain't wearing a rock."

I winced. It was true—my left fourth finger wore only a simple gold band. When Richard made his haphazard proposal he hadn't gotten around to buying me a ring. After I gently reminded him of the engagement ring convention, he gamely offered to buy me one and we spent an afternoon ring shopping. But the one ring we saw that I really wanted, an Art Deco cocktail number, was well out of our budget. I felt ashamed for having such extravagant desires, and guilty that Richard—my kindhearted Richard—might feel he wasn't able to meet them. So I told Richard that I couldn't settle on a style, and tried to convince myself that it wasn't so important. I told myself it all made sense, but I found myself eyeing the ostentatious engagement rings at Hasharama. My eyes involuntarily settled on Gigi's huge diamond, which showed well in the light of Dr. Phil's on-screen image.

"Means you're true to yourself," Gigi explained. "You got your own drummer."

I nodded, unconvinced.

She looked at me intently and said, "We got married six months ago."

I was surprised that it had all happened so fast and so recently, but I couldn't see why that was a problem. "I believe in love at first sight," I volunteered.

Gigi looked flustered in a way I had never imagined she could. She made strange faces and gestures with her hands, as she shouted, "I'm *seven and a half* months pregnant!"

"So?" I started. "It's a technicality. Lots of women get pregnant before—"

"I was *dating!*" she interrupted me. "I practically slept my way through the entire trading floor of Morgan Sachs! I mean, I'm not ashamed of what I did. But I ain't no Sister Mary Bag of Doughnuts. I didn't know then that my Milton was *my* Milton!"

She stared at me so unrelentingly that I had to blink several times. Then she once again swore me to absolute secrecy. I was to exhume my mother and slice out her eyeballs if I should ever reveal the truth.

"The truth is I'm not sure who the father of my baby is." She caressed her belly, as if apologizing directly to her child. "There was this other guy. John. We dated a few times, nothing exclusive. At first I was kind of dazzled by him. I mean, he was gorgeous. Like a John John type, ya know? He'd order up a helicopter and we'd fly off for a romantic weekend. Talk about *class!*" She smiled at the memory. Then a frown crossed her face. "He was a real charmer," she continued. "But it was always weird. We were meeting in strange places, staying in hotels. He never introduced me to any of his friends." She sighed. "I think he was seeing somebody else. And you know what?"

"What?"

"I was happy to get rid of that mess. Like he could take me to Paris for the weekend, but he couldn't meet me on the corner for a Coke and a slice? So I made up my mind it was gonna be Milton, and we got married. Then when I found out I was pregnant, I did the math, and . . ."

Gigi grabbed my arm and dug her fingers in. "John kept saying how much he wanted to have a baby," she whispered urgently. "He wouldn't use a condom. Said nothing should come between us. And I let him. I got caught up . . ." She faltered and was silent a few moments. "I think if John finds out I'm pregnant, he's going to want to claim he's the father," she said. "He's going to tell every- body, and my Milton is going to leave me." She looked at me. Even though we were both pregnant, she seemed twice as large as me— in fact, she openly boasted that she now topped two hundred pounds. "This has to be Milton's baby," she said, almost pleading.

I didn't know what to say, so I held out my arms and we hugged each other over our bellies. I was rooting for Milton too. A crack had opened up in her brash Queens persona and she sud- denly seemed very lonely. I saw that she really did need a friend, and I hoped it would be me.

4

The life of a modern-day elephant is stressful and complicated.

—LAURENT DE BRUNHOFF, *BABAR'S YOGA FOR ELEPHANTS*

On a Wednesday afternoon in July, Cedar Hill seemed like the Eden of Central Park.

At the top of the grassy slope, lovers cavorted under the dappled sunlight of breezy trees. Couples sipped lemonade, read books side by side, and idled arm in arm under the sheltering sky. At the bottom of the hill, on the other side of a small green fence, lay a meadow full of the inevitable consequences of so much love. It teemed with dozens of infants—some too small to leave their strollers, others crawling in circles around their caregivers, still more stumbling gleefully on the grass. On a bench near the fence,

I sat rubbing my belly with sunscreen, wondering, *When was the last time Richard and I rolled in the grass and sipped lemonade?* He was supposed to have been here with me today. But he said he needed to catch up on his "early Wittgenstein" for an academic paper. "I'm working on the problem of solipsism," he said somewhat vaguely from his usual position on the couch.

From my position on the bench, I had a loge-ticket view of the playground for some of New York's best-bred tots, the spawn of Park Avenue socialites and captains of industry. Of course, the captains and socialites were elsewhere—an army of nannies tended to their offspring instead. Pregnancy had turned me into a baby hound. In my preprocreative days, I was too absorbed in my love life and nightlife to have any interest in the arcana of child development. Like most of my self-involved peers, I thought of babies as screaming vegetables that promptly turned into bratty schoolkids much as caterpillars become butterflies. Now that I was about to have a little vegetable of my own, babies had become a source of endless fascination and analysis. After months of scrutinizing every passing stroller and interviewing new mothers at the local parks, I fancied myself a baby connoisseur. I could spot the difference between a four-month-old and a seven-month-old, between a temporarily displeased infant and one with a personality disorder.

As I sat on my bench sizing up the tots, a pregnant woman wearing wide Chanel sunglasses sauntered up to me. Gold bangles jangled against her stainless steel Rolex. She flicked her curly platinum locks back with her hand. It was one of our sometime yoga colleagues, Jessica, the designer blond. She was not part of our lunch group, and, truth be told, I was glad. "Do you mind if I sit down?" she asked, lowering herself next to me before I had a chance to answer.

When I'd first been introduced to her a couple of months before, Jessica's attitude toward me had been dismissive. But ever since she'd figured out that our pal Susan was in fact *the* Mrs. Harcourt Fielding, whose husband's family name was listed on the boards of many major philanthropic institutions, she'd been a lot friendlier toward me and the other yoga mamas.

"Look what Steve surprised me with last weekend," she said, and held up a diamond solitaire on a slender chain around her neck for me to see. "Do you like it?"

"Wow," I said. "Is it a baby present?"

"Baby present? You mean a *pushing* present?" Jessica sounded incredulous. "Oh, no, this is just a *snack!* I've got my eye on a tennis bracelet at Cartier. It's expensive but, you know." She smirked. "Steve is very competitive."

Jessica reminded me a little too much of Jennifer—the platinum sociopath that Len, an ex-boyfriend, left me for. Len was before Richard. He was the lead singer of an alt-rock band that was always on the verge of making it big. We met at a *College Music Journal* showcase at the Mercury Lounge. PJ Harvey was heading the bill, and every guy in the city with a thing for moody, dark-haired girls was there. Len was at the bar, all skinny and cool in a vintage Dead Boys T-shirt and black jeans. When he said, "I like your walk," in his disarming way, I paused. Then I replied, "Thanks. I like your tattoo." We were together for two-and-a-half stormy years. He dumped me because he "wasn't ready for a relationship." A week later I spied him at Café Habana with Jennifer, whom I had always thought of as everything that is wrong with the human race. Jessica reminded me of Jennifer, not just for her vapid smile and Botticelli hair but also because they were both shameless social climbers. Jennifer worked a different hierarchy, though—she stomped on Len in order to meet Seal's guitarist.

Jessica turned her attention to the scene in front of us. "Are you here to check out the nannies? Cedar Hill is *the* place to scout for one."

I said I wasn't in the market.

"Oh, I see," Jessica said.

She glanced up at the buildings on Fifth Avenue overlooking the park. "Can you imagine living in one of those," she said, pointing up to the penthouses with park views. "Heaven!"

The idea had never occurred to me. I suppose I must have known that people lived in those apartments—I just never pictured myself in one of them.

Jessica said she and her husband would soon be moving into the "Pork House." Before developers turned it into a luxury condo, it had been a sausage factory. "It's the best building in TriBeCa," she proclaimed. In the meantime, they were living in a temporary Soho rental as contractors finished renovations. "We've spent a fortune redoing the place," she said. "Got to make room for baby!"

Carving out a baby room wasn't easy, she let me know, because the loft had "only 3,000 square feet." I quickly calculated that that was about five times the size of the concrete cave that Richard and I inhabited. I started to fantasize about a nursery the size of a basketball court. The baby would need a map to get from one end to the other.

Jessica started to tick off the features that were missing from the apartment when they bought it: It had no steam room, no sauna, no Jacuzzi, and no central air-conditioning. "The kitchen was so nineties. And I don't even want to *talk* about the window treatments," she added—although talk about them she did, and for some time.

Then Jessica turned the tables and started probing me on my living arrangements. Richard and I live in the tallest, widest, and ugliest complex in our part of Manhattan. When I mentioned our address, she drew a blank. "I never noticed those buildings," she said. "They're very convenient, a great location," I said, feeling defensive. Richard, I knew, would have had a more distanced take on Jessica. I could almost hear him sniff at her: "Aspirational." But Richard wasn't here.

We sat in silence for a few moments.

"Have you ordered your stroller yet?" Jessica asked. "I just got mine."

I looked across the sea of nannies and tots and I noticed that many of the strollers were identical—a fancy Italian brand. So far, I had failed to make sense of all the strollers on offer.

"No," I replied. "Does it look like these?" I gestured toward the strollers in the grass.

"A *Peg Pérego?*" she said, sounding scandalized. "I live in TriBeCa! I got a Bugaboo Frog."

Now that I thought about it, she was right. All the downtown mommies pushed around the big-wheeled Bugaboo, which looked to me like a lunar landing module. Women like Jessica seem to have access to some sort of secret female information-sharing club—they know the right handbag, the right place to get your hair done, the right stroller. But the Frog, I knew, cost $700. The Pérego was a steal by comparison at $350. On the other hand, as Richard had pointed out, you could get a decent stroller for $80 at Kmart.

"Why the Frog?" I asked, half in jest, half in desperation.

"Because if you don't have one, all the other mommies get together and kick you out of the playground," Jessica said with a laugh.

I smiled uneasily. Whenever I had worried about whether Richard and I could afford a baby, I'd always reassured myself that the only things we really needed were two breasts and a sink. Apparently it was a bit more complicated.

"Of course, if we ever move uptown, we'll get a Peg Pérego," Jessica said thoughtfully, her gaze shifting back to the Fifth Avenue penthouses. "You know, this neighborhood has some great schools. We might have to move here when we grow up. So," she said, turning to me with a portentous air, "have you thought about where you're sending your child to preschool? We've reserved a spot for an interview at Metropolitan," she said, patting her round belly. "In New York, it's *all* about the reservation."

I felt a hot stab of anxiety. I fidgeted on the bench, shading my eyes. I hadn't thought about it. I hadn't even done any research—was preschool the same thing as nursery school? How could it be that I knew the lyrics to every Blondie song ever recorded, but I didn't know the first thing about toddler education? I was a bad mother already. "That's great," I stuttered. "How did you decide on Metropolitan?"

"Oh, it's *the* place," Jessica said warmly. "They really know the difference between a twenty-two-month-old and a twenty-six-month-old. And all the celebrities send their kids there. I mean, if you have to take your kid on a playdate, wouldn't you rather do it at Cindy Crawford's house?" Then she added, "Of course, our son still has to get past the interview."

I struggled to imagine my unborn daughter at the age of two, answering her interview questions wearing a tiny sash and a swimsuit.

"Anyway, I've already volunteered for the social committee." Jessica winked. "Sometimes you've got to put out a little bit. We really want Metropolitan because it's a feeder school for Saint Sebastian Academy."

It sounded vaguely familiar. "Isn't that an all-boys school?" I asked.

"The best on the East Coast." She nodded. "We signed up as soon as I found out I was pregnant. It's very competitive and the list fills up so fast. Especially for the boarding candidates."

Jessica's son was not even born yet, and already she'd packed his bags and sent him off to boarding school? She must have caught a look on my face.

"Oh, it's only an hour away. And the boys can come home on the weekends." She lowered her voice. "I'm sure you know Susan's husband, Harcourt, is on the board of Metropolitan."

I didn't have the slightest idea about Harcourt's influence at Metropolitan. Susan never talked about things like that.

"I hear from some of the ladies on the social committee that Harcourt can really help with the admissions process," she said, choosing her words carefully. Jessica gave me a searching look. "If you know what I mean."

I was determined not to know what she meant. I retreated into silence.

"Listen, I know it can be tough figuring out this school thing, especially in your, um, situation," Jessica said. "If you need any help, anything, just shout." She stood up to the sound of jangling bangles. "Well, I'm going to check out the scenery," she said, "I think I've found my nanny!"

She wandered off into the meadow, tiptoeing among the nannies, who seemed to register her presence with subtle changes in tone and stance. Some glanced defensively at their charges, others suddenly took to wiping imaginary scraps of detritus from the children's faces. One nanny who had earlier shown zero interest in her one-year-old ward suddenly started chirping out the ABCs.

Jessica honed in on a lone nanny sitting on the grass with a blond boy about two years old, who was wearing Ralph Lauren head to toe. The nanny was matronly, neatly dressed, and strikingly well-groomed. To her side stood a luxury convertible four-wheel-drive Peg Pérego, equipped with what looked like a refrigeration compartment. They chatted amicably for some time. It seemed to go well.

Meanwhile, on the bench, I was stewing in the juices of prenatal anxiety. While the rest of my baby's generation would ride their shiny carriages up to the top of New York society, I thought, my poor, deprived daughter would spend her infancy tied to my chest with a soiled blanket. She'd end up a homeschooled freak with no friends and a disgusting insect collection.

When I got home, I dialed the Metropolitan preschool.

"I'm interested in registering my daughter for classes," I said.

"Date of birth?" the young woman who answered said laconically.

"Well, she's not quite there yet. . . ."

Pause. "Excuse me?"

"I mean, she's due in two months—nine and a half weeks, actually."

"I'm sorry, we don't take prebirth reservations." Her tone of voice was dismissive, and I hung up, frustrated. I was sure I wasn't getting the whole story—*Jessica* had managed to get in on a prebirth plan. I decided to call back under a different identity. Mentally preparing myself by pretending that I was in a cavernous penthouse with park views, I cooked up an English accent for good measure. The same, bored woman answered my call. "I'm curious about your preschool offerings," I said, pleased with my posh accent.

"Date of birth?"

I led her to believe that my daughter was a sprightly three-month-old.

"Address?"

I gave her the details.

She paused. "Downtown," she said, skepticism audible in her voice. "Tell me about her current arrangements."

"Well, she has *loads* of toys," I began.

"No, I mean, who is taking care of her?" she said impatiently.

"Oh, I see, I am . . . but I get lots of help from . . . from Emma, our governess. Emma is so . . . smashing!" I was never a very good liar.

I heard only a contemptuous silence.

"How may I register?" I asked.

"You have to take a tour first." It sounded like she was giving the explanation for the hundredth time.

"May I register for the tour?"

"No. You have to call on the first Wednesday of September, between ten A.M. and eleven A.M."

"Is this the number I call?"

"No."

I imagined a telephone number that connected its dialers with the private school equivalent of CIA headquarters, to be answered by a team of voice analyzers in white Chanel lab coats who pinpoint the exact pedigree of the caller through her vocal inflections and determine the square footage of her apartment by measuring traces of echo. "How do I get the number?" My vowels were starting to flatten out.

"You have to send in a preapplication form first, and then we will send you the number. The preapplication fee is one hundred fifty dollars."

I tried to stay in character. "May I request one of the preapplication forms?"

"I believe they have all been reserved. You've left it a little late."

"Late?" I said, starting to sound distinctly stateside. "Are you sure—"

"Well, there *is* a diversity policy," she admitted grudgingly. "And you do live downtown. But these forms haven't been available for some time, so I wouldn't count on it."

"Since when have all the forms been reserved?" I asked, getting huffy.

"Oh, six months or so."

Now I was furious. I couldn't get a preapplication form to get the number to sign up for the tour to apply for a space in the preschool because my real daughter wasn't born yet, but my imaginary daughter couldn't get in because all the preapplication forms were taken up before she was supposedly born! There was no way in!

"So how much does the program cost?" I asked, dropping all pretense of Englishness.

"The five-day nine A.M. to twelve A.M. program is $26,250."

I slammed down the phone.

I was shaking. I glanced around our cramped apartment. As usual, it was a disaster. Dirty clothes and newspapers littered the floor. Dishes overflowed in the sink and colonized every surface of our tiny kitchen.

Richard poked his shaggy head through the door. He was wearing his favorite plaid flannel shirt, which made him look less like a professor of European history and more like the farm boy he really was. "Hey there, gorgeous," he said. I looked at the strapping, artlessly sexy young man I'd fallen in love with. "Our daughter is going to grow up to be a coupon clipper," I sobbed.

"What?"

"We can't afford to send her to preschool, and she can't get in anyway!"

"But she hasn't been born yet."

"I know!" I threw my arms up in despair. "We'll never get the preapplication form for the secret phone number for the tour!"

He had no idea what I was talking about, but he put his hand on my shoulder and said, "We'll find a school, Laura."

"But Metropolitan is a feeder school!"

"Feeder school? She's not a cow, you know," he said.

"Yes, but to get into Saint Sebastian's—"

"Saint Sebastian's? Isn't that a boy's school?" He laughed gently.

"Whatever!" I said. "She's going to end up in some crappy public high school in a classroom with sixty other kids and she'll hang out with drug-addicted freaks!"

He gave me a great big bear hug. "Our daughter will get the best education in the world," he said soothingly. "After all, she'll be lucky enough to have you for a mother. Now you just rest and keep her baking in the oven."

"Baking in the oven." I loved that.

To other men, I may have been intense, "difficult," whatever. But ever since that first day in my graduate school seminar on Medieval Narratives, when Richard strolled in and casually took the seat next to me, I knew I'd finally met someone who considered me his happy fate. When Richard looked at me he saw mom, apple pie, the promise of domestic bliss. He stroked my hair, and suddenly I felt safe again.

"Besides," Richard added, "it's the prep schools that have the drug problems. There are plenty of great public schools. And our girl is going to be a little Einstein. She'll get a scholarship, and that will solve all our problems."

That was so Richard. An academic scholarship had been his ticket out of the rinky town of Roundup, Montana. He had no doubt that his daughter would have every opportunity to succeed in just the same way. I wasn't so sure, but I was content to take cover under his confidence.

"Anyway," he said, "I've brought home a surprise."

From a shopping bag he retrieved a Baby Monitor—a microphone-headphone set that promised to let you "hear your baby's first moments." I lay down on the bed and we went searching for our mysterious little pupil-to-be. We put the microphone everywhere on my belly but all we heard were strange whooshes, gurgles, and thumps. At one point I was sure I heard the pumping of her tiny heart, but Richard listened in and insisted I was just passing gas.

It didn't matter. Every now and then, our baby gave a hearty kick against my round belly or twisted her little body in a somersault and we laughed with delight. Richard tried communicating with her in Morse code—he had read somewhere about a fetus that responded to two taps with two taps back.

"I think she's talking," he said excitedly. "See? She's going to ace her SATs! Forget preschool, she's going straight to Harvard!"

I giggled sheepishly.

Then he gave up on the tapping and started singing a song to her through my belly wall.

5

I believe that we're doing yoga
so that we can be strong enough to be fragile.

—RODNEY YEE, *YOGA: THE POETRY OF THE BODY*

Isla and I sat on a bench outside the hospital waiting for Antonio to pick us up.

Richard and Antonio had both come up with excuses to get out of the required seminar on the birthing process, so Isla and I decided to go together. The session had reminded me of nothing so much as the pretakeoff lectures from flight attendants. And in every plane crash I've ever heard of, it didn't make a damn bit of difference whether anyone knew where the emergency exit was—they were still going down in flames.

When Antonio pulled up in his black Hummer, we were trading

jokes about all the catastrophic deliveries we'd heard of. We were slouching, so my head was about even with Isla's, but her legs seemed to extend yards beyond the tips of my toes. In the bright sun, her rich skin glowed as though she'd been dipped in gold. Antonio was wearing his business uniform: a tailored jacket, trendy blue jeans, and a gold Panerai watch. Tall, good-looking, and approaching forty, he was one of those men who had handled the discovery of a receding hairline by shaving everything off, leaving only a fashionable trace of stubble.

"It's amazing," he said, pecking my cheek. "You girls are pregnant and you still look like you're ready for the nightclubs!"

I reflexively tilted my head to its best viewing angle. Antonio was a curious mix of a working-class Italian-American childhood and Columbia Business School. He could sound as sophisticated and exacting as one of Richard's academic supervisors; yet when he wanted to be funny, he laid on a thick New Jersey accent. And he was also slightly thuggish: the kind of guy, I thought, who'd make a woman tattoo "Tony's bitch #173" on her ass if he could.

"Come on, *macho,* let us get in the car," said Isla, rolling her eyes skyward.

I sprawled across the backseat, and we pulled away. Isla had invited me for lunch at her loft, and I'd jumped at the chance. With its chic custom-made furniture and expansive Hudson River vistas, lounging there made me feel fabulous.

All of a sudden, she said sharply, "Where are you going?"

Antonio had been driving west and was now headed back downtown.

"I know a shortcut," he replied, annoyed. "Over to the West Side Highway."

"Don't you go that way!" Isla shouted. "You are going to make us lost again!"

"Give me a break, woman," he said. He yanked the car off to the left onto a side street. Isla gritted her teeth. Within moments, sure enough, we were stuck in traffic on the grid of streets that feed the Holland Tunnel. Isla started muttering in rapid-fire Spanish. My high school Spanish is good, although some of the curses were new to me. "You are unsupportable!" she was saying. "Don't you ever listen to anyone? Typical! You man-goat! You caterpillar-sucking imbecile!" Or at least that's what it sounded like.

He glared at her and gunned the motor.

"Just fine," she said, exhaling loudly. "You just do whatever you want to. You only think about yourself. I am not going to fight with you this time. I just feel sorry for you." She looked out the window, her nose in the air suggesting a feigned indifference that convinced no one. "Of course, I know why she calls you 'Little *Tito,*'" she sniffed, as if to herself.

"You leave my mother out of this, you crazy bitch!" Antonio yelled.

The invectives flared back and forth between the front seats. Then the traffic cleared and the West Side Highway opened before us. Like a passing tropical storm, the argument ended just as quickly as it had started, and the two chatted and joked the rest of the way back as though nothing had happened. I was the only one still shaking when we finally arrived at Greene Street.

Isla and Antonio were what you could call a "fighting couple": If they ever stopped fighting, they would quickly fall out of love. I had lived that way once, with Len. We didn't even wait until we finished making love before we started trying to chew each other to pieces. Richard's acceptance of me had been such a reassuring contrast to those insecure days. But lately, whenever I expressed my worries about having a child, and Richard would blithely reassure me that everything would turn out all right, it seemed he didn't grasp what was really at stake. And when I tried to pick a fight with him about it, he wouldn't fight back. He'd retreat into a glass bubble with his books and thoughts, and I simply couldn't get through.

Antonio dropped us off. Leaning out the window of his mammoth driving machine, he put a gentle hand on Isla's arm and said, "Baby, you know the gallerist is coming by to do some estimates for the auction—make sure you let him in."

"Of course, I will let him in," she said with a snort. Isla had told me about Antonio's art collection and had mentioned he was planning to sell a few pieces.

She nodded at the doorman, then led me into the elegant industrial lobby. We stepped into one of the oversize elevators and she unlocked her floor.

Isla's place was a decorator's wet dream. Straight lines along the walls and floors extended almost to the horizon, punctuated by artful arrangements of minimalist furniture and works of art. Three or four mono-color rugs scattered across the acres of polished wood flooring seemed intended only to emphasize the impossibility of covering such a vast tract of land. The paintings, to my uneducated eye, counted as "contemporary"—that is, they involved broad splashes of shape and color that almost looked like something familiar, but not quite. In other places, black-and-white portraits of beautiful or striking people were grouped together. A few were of Isla. I thought I recognized Elsa Schiaparelli and Coco Chanel, but I wasn't sure. At the other end of the main room, a wall of warehouse-sized windows offered views of the Hudson. Overhead, a pyramidal skylight illuminated the space from above.

Nothing was out of place. Even the soft mohair throws on the sofas were meticulously folded, as though part of a store display. If Richard and I were let loose, the countertops would be strewn with newspapers, there would be wet rings from teacups on the glass coffee tables, and the floor would be littered with socks and shoes, allowed to fall wherever they had been kicked off. I marveled at Isla and Antonio's discipline. They seemed to maintain a level of orderliness that I would have thought unattainable without a squadron of housekeepers—which, I realized on second thought, was exactly what Isla and Antonio had.

I lowered myself sideways onto a low-riding Italian sofa that made up in attitude what it lacked in back support. I pointed to a framed snapshot of an elegant, dark-haired woman in her fifties that was on a side table. She was wearing pearl earrings and a black cardigan and was standing on a rocky beach. She looked a bit like an older, rougher version of Isla. "Is that your mother?" I asked.

"Yes," she said, "she is in Spain. I visit her there, but it is so dull. In Spain, all the girls are happy just to have a nice house and a stupid husband with a job. For me, I needed something more in life."

Isla sat down and began to speak of her mother. I had always imagined that Isla had grown up in a luxurious hacienda, taming wild horses and dancing to guitar music. But in fact her mother was a very poor woman from a small village whose dream was to become a flight attendant. At nineteen, she got a job as a receptionist at a resort hotel. "But when she became pregnant with me, the hotel told her that she cannot work there anymore," Isla said. Isla never knew her father, although a vicious cousin once whispered to her that he was the mayor of their old village, who also owned the hotel. "That is Spain," she said with a shrug, "thirty years ago."

Shunned by her own family, Isla's mother waited until she gave birth, then packed up her infant daughter and her belongings and left. She eventually found jobs cleaning hotel rooms in Torremolinos, Marbella, and finally in the Canary Islands, on the craggy, black mound of congealed lava called Lanzarote.

"The Spanish say that God forgot about Lanzarote on the seventh day of creation," she said. "That is why nothing lives there."

On Lanzarote, her mother started baby-sitting for tourists, and eventually became a nanny for the island's wealthy families. Isla finally started attending school. She was a good foot taller than all the other girls, and she thought of herself as a freak. She was always trying to persuade her classmates, "Let us sit down somewhere so we can talk!" She hated sticking out above everyone else, like a weed. Sometimes when she came home from school, her mother would look at her as she ducked her head through the doorway of their tiny apartment and burst into tears, wailing, "How much taller are you going to get?"

Then one day, while Isla was walking alone on a black sand beach, she was "spotted." A fast-talking man with a neatly trimmed goatee approached her. She thought he was hitting on her, so she ignored him. But he followed her at a distance for an entire afternoon until she went home to her mother. He was a modeling agency executive on vacation, and he promised them the world. He started calling her "Isla," and the name stuck. "My real name is Maria Asuncion," she said to me, as if revealing a secret. "But nobody uses my real name anymore."

She was sixteen years old when she landed in Madrid. Within a year she had moved to Milan, then Paris. At twenty-one, after her first cover for American *Vogue,* she moved to New York City. She was modest, but I could tell she had been near the top of her field. She'd lived on a carousel of international travel, catwalk appearances, photo shoots, and industry parties.

I would never have predicted that I'd befriend someone like her.

It was not just that I'd never been to a catwalk show in my life—although I *was* secretly a reader of fashion magazines. It was that the physical laws governing her universe were so different from those of my own. In the world of advertising copywriters, I had always been considered something of a hottie—mainly because the standards were so pathetically low. But Isla had the kind of looks that open a different class of doors altogether. Antonio fell in love with Isla before he met her, while perusing a copy of *Elle* magazine. There she was, frolicking on the beach in St. Barths wearing that season's abbreviated swimwear. He vowed that someday she'd be his. "Antonio is such an operator." She smiled wryly as she recalled their courtship. "He always had a girl on his arm, always some pretty little model. When he saw my picture, he asked his girlfriend to invite a group of her friends to his restaurant. You know, she was at the same agency as me. As soon as I come to the restaurant, he just ignores her. He was so tacky!" She rolled her eyes. "I figured him out pretty fast."

At first, Isla fiercely resisted Antonio's overtures. He seemed too eager and a little sleazy. When she saw him at a party, she'd hand him her drink, tell him to go fill it up, and then walk away. If I'd pulled a diva game like that on Richard he would have shrugged his shoulders and given up.

But when Isla went to Europe for the fall collections, Antonio followed. She would run into him in the restaurants of Milan, the private clubs of London. In Paris, he somehow managed to score front-row seats to all her catwalk shows. She told him she was in love with someone else, which was a lie. He told her she was in love with him and just didn't know it yet. She didn't know what to think. Then, finally, she opened the door to her hotel bedroom in Barcelona, and he came in to stay.

"He has dated some of the most beautiful women in the world," Isla said. "And then he wanted me. I thought, he must love me for who I am."

She'd been the elusive one, and he'd relished the chase.

"That is men," Isla said, pouring glasses of iced tea from a tall pitcher. But then she frowned and sighed. "Maybe he was excited by the challenge. You know, I did not make it so easy for him. I made him work hard for it. Maybe it was not worth the effort."

"Of course it was, Isla," I said. "Antonio clearly loves you." From the way he smiled at her, the way he had just kissed her when he said good-bye, I knew his love was more than skin deep. "Besides," I said, gesturing around the apartment, "you guys have made a beautiful life together."

"I let him decorate the place however he wants," she said dismissively.

They kept strictly separate accounts. The paintings and furnishings were his; the loft was hers. Every month they tallied receipts and divided expenses down the middle. My mind drifted toward the perilous state of Richard's and my finances. One of the advantages of having nothing, I realized, is that at least you don't have to fight about how to divide it.

"Of course, now he is going to sell some of his collection, because he has to pay for Extra Virgin."

Extra Virgin was getting deep fried by the critics. The *New York Times* food writer complained of an "excessively unctuous host, oleaginous fish, and slimy clientele." I guessed that Antonio's career had already crested. In his twenties and thirties, he had surfed culinary trends to the heights of success; approaching forty, he was probably considered an old-timer who had lost his edge.

A suspicious look crossed Isla's face. She was slow to trust, and I could see that a part of her regretted telling me as much about her past as she had. I didn't want to push her, so I changed the subject. I asked her how her modeling work was going.

"It is not going," she said flatly. "I have done some maternity shoots so that they don't forget about me. But there is not much money. My agent is always asking me how much do I weigh. But I am pregnant—how am I supposed to have a baby and *not* get big?"

To ordinary human eyes, Isla still looked astonishingly fit and slender, even with her bulging midriff. I had already gained over thirty pounds—and only six or seven of that would be baby.

"He is always bothering me about exercise, diet, exercise, diet." She closed her eyes. "Anyway, everyone knows that a woman cannot be a model for her whole life."

She said it like she was making an offhand observation, but in between her meticulously groomed brows I saw the trace of a vertical line. She was thirty-three years old, an age when many people are only beginning their real careers, and hers had already peaked. I had thought of Isla as someone who had won the lottery, but for her, I realized the future was just an empty plain. She was probably convinced Antonio would disappear along with the photographers and fashion groupies. She would end up alone, with no education and few career prospects, raising a child just as her mother did, on her own.

"Now that we are like married people, all I wear is this," Isla continued, indicating the T-shirt covering half her belly. "Do you think Antonio will continue to think that I am exciting?"

"Are you kidding?" I said. "Look at you! You're eight months pregnant and you still get guys following you down the street."

It was true. Walking past a group of men with Isla was like walking into a playground with an armful of cotton candy.

"Sometimes when we fight I think about throwing him out. I want to say to him, 'You gave me a baby, now leave me alone.' Anyway, I am like a country that he has already conquered. Soon he will get bored with me and will look for a new world to challenge him."

I tried to protest, but she insisted it was true. "Don't you ever worry for yourself?" she asked. "When you become a mother, you have no power over your husband."

"Who, Richard?" I asked uncertainly. I tried to imagine Richard flirting with someone else. I scanned my memories of the faces of the women I'd met at his faculty parties. I found it difficult to believe that he would have found any of them attractive. Seventeenth-century Dutch history just didn't seem to bring in the campus beauties. Did any of his colleagues think of him as a hot number? Had they tried to lure him into bed with discussions of Spinoza's views on the mind/body problem? Instead of provoking jealousy, the idea made me laugh. After two years of peaceful coexistence, Richard and I were a fixed part of each other's lives. I had a lot of things to worry about, but Richard running off with a saucy professor wasn't one of them.

We started talking about the other yoga mamas. Isla seemed especially keen to uncover problems in their relationships. Margaret, with her absentee partner, seemed to offer the most abject lesson in male unreliability. "She is so alone," Isla said.

I had to agree.

"And what about Susan and her story about the seashells? Have you ever seen Harcourt in person?" Isla asked. "Does *she* ever see Harcourt?"

None of the yoga mamas had met him yet, and whenever we asked Susan what he was up to, she said he was on a business trip. Then Isla eyed me searchingly, and asked, "And what about Gigi? You know about her secret, yes?"

I froze. Gigi had told me no one else knew, and she had made me swear to keep her secret safe. I felt a twinge of jealousy—*Gigi confided in Isla too?* I thought she had singled me out in the group as the only one she could really trust. Perhaps our friendship wasn't that special to her after all? I mumbled I wasn't sure if I knew. But from my red face and embarrassed tones I was certain Isla could see I was hiding something.

She widened her eyes. "Gigi and Milton only started to see each other *eight* months ago. . . ." She trailed off and looked at me questioningly.

I felt the sharp sting of humiliation. "I know," I blurted. "But she left the other guy before she found out she was pregnant!"

Isla's already enormous eyes expanded. "There was *another* guy?"

There was no way out. Isla peppered me with questions. At first, I refused to answer. Then she more or less pieced the story together, adding one or two egregious details of her own invention. Along the way, Isla's worst fears about men seemed to be confirmed—initiating another round of bizarre invectives. "That bastard pig-licker!" she kept repeating in Spanish. Finally, I told her everything.

I had betrayed one of my new best friends. But it was a relief to bring someone else into the circle. I made Isla swear to tell no one. "Do not worry," she reassured me. "I can imagine what Gigi is feeling, and, you and me, we are not going to make it any more hard for her. We are going to help her."

I wondered if I could really trust her to keep Gigi's secret.

And I tried to convince myself that I had made an honest mistake.

6

Why settle for just physical results when you could
have Cosmic Consciousness?
Why settle for a banana when you could have nirvana?

—SHARON GANNON AND DAVID LIFE, *JIVAMUKTI YOGA*

As the clock ticked down toward my due date, I felt a strange mixture of excitement and foreboding. On the one hand, I was longing to meet my daughter. At home, I spent hours organizing the crib and the changing table, shuffling around the tiny diapers, ointments, and burp cloths. I lingered over adorable hand-me-downs from thoughtful relatives, and then carefully re-laundered the garments with "infant-safe" detergent. I pictured myself holding my baby girl in my arms and telling her how much I loved her, and listening to her coo gently in response. And I looked forward to retiring the maternity jeans and blouses that I was sick of wearing every day and returning to my old, familiar shape.

On the other hand, with only eight weeks to go, I wasn't quite ready. I was frightened by the prospect of squeezing a child out of my body, and even more afraid of the uncertainties of life once she arrived. Sometimes I lay immobile on my bed and wished time would stop.

But my biggest worry these days was Richard. As birth approached, the argument about our daughter-to-be's name had heated up. Hannah or Anna, to me, were the kind of names that marked one out as a dutiful taxpayer and a knitter of tea cozies. I wanted to give her a name that was unique and original. I'd always felt misrepresented by the blandness of my own moniker, and had secretly wished for something more dramatic. Maybe if my parents had called me "Seraphina" or "Delilah" I'd have cut a dashing figure on the world's stage—I'd be writing brilliant screenplays and yacht-hopping in Capri, instead of wasting my weekends in college on the couch making mix tapes or chasing pretentious losers at the clubs. Back then, I'd fantasized about changing my name, but ultimately decided that it was already too late. I was a lifetime Laura heading toward grad school.

But it wasn't too late for my daughter.

Whenever I proposed an appropriately original name, Richard would shoot it down, accusing me of wanting to stigmatize our daughter. I tried "Emmeline," arguing that it had heroic antecedents, such as Emmeline Pankhurst, the early suffragette. He could even give her the nickname "Emma," safe and classic. Richard eyed me coldly and muttered, "Lunatic." He stomped out of the house, saying, "We are *not* naming our daughter after a song by the Ohio Players!"

For the first time in our relationship, we were facing an irresolvable conflict.

My ordinarily accommodating husband was unmoving. He rejected my first choice, then my second, then my third, then every suggestion thereafter. "You can call her Hannah or Anna," he kept repeating.

I felt a growing sense of panic. One evening, during yet another one of our name arguments, I actually had a wild impulse to jump out the window. I grabbed the wall to steady myself, and remembered a conversation I'd had one night with my ex, Len. "Do you think you'll ever want kids?" I'd asked him tentatively. "Let's have four!" he'd replied. "And if we have a girl," he'd said, "I want to name her Persephone." Len hadn't even been close to husband-and-father material. But as I thought back on the qualities in him that I had once cherished—his playfulness, his originality—I asked myself whether we hadn't been soul mates after all. Richard was a steadier partner, but he could be rigid. Right then I wondered what I had given up to be with him.

As I neared my due date, my anxiety intensified. I'd wake up in the middle of the night and reach for my stack of name books, desperately seeking an entry that would offer some sort of compromise. But Richard vetoed each suggestion with the bullying certainty of a man who knows he'll get his way. One afternoon, I slipped a Pixies disc in the compact CD player I'd nestled among the diapers and ointments on our daughter's changing table and started bouncing my big belly to the beat. Richard got up and replaced my disc with Mozart.

"Better for baby," he said.

On a sweltering day at the Healthy Harvest, after a grueling yoga session in which Gaia had made one too many unreasonable demands on my body, I sat glumly with the yoga mamas, turning over impossible baby names in my head. The other women's company was usually enough to draw me out of my funk, but today it didn't seem to be working for any of us. We were all wearing late pregnancy clothes—below-the-knee skirts with stretchy front panels and tent-sized T-shirts. The bra I was wearing—two sizes larger than any I had worn before getting pregnant—was starting to cut into my back, and there were strange painful twinges in my hip ligaments. Gigi was unusually quiet as she contemplated her ever-expanding belly. Susan fussed with her food, gingerly moving to the side any vegetables that looked overcooked or non-organic. Isla made more sour comments about the feckless Antonio and her unfeeling agent, Jean-Claude, although she lacked the energy to pursue either subject. Margaret listlessly reviewed the latest about the missing father of her child. Apparently he'd secured a job with the firm Stiffshirt and Whiteshoe— or something like that—and had sent notice of his new position to everyone in his old firm except for her. Then he tried to poach one of her clients. Adding to Margaret's bitterness were the snide comments she overheard from fellow workers. Although she was planning to take only six weeks of maternity leave, some of her male partners were already whispering about the "mommy track."

Gigi tried to perk us up. "Girls, we've got to get it together," she said. "Look at us, we're about to have babies! It's the happiest time in our lives and we're acting like somebody died."

"You are right," said Isla. "I don't know what is the matter with me. Maybe I need to go to a place where I can relax."

Susan put a carrot down and spoke up. "We have to go to Le Refuge!"

By now, we all knew the story about Le Refuge, the luxurious spa-hotel on Long Island, where Susan and her husband, Harcourt, had spent their honeymoon more than nine years ago. The fateful strip of sand on which Susan and Harcourt found their matching shellfish and discovered true love belonged to Le Refuge, located not far from Harcourt's family's ancestral estate in the Hamptons. When Harcourt invited Susan for an organic juice blend on their very first date, it was to the bar at Le Refuge that he took her. When they wedded, there was no discussion about where to have the ceremony: It had to be Le Refuge.

Even though there wasn't the remotest chance that Richard and I could afford a single night's stay at Le Refuge, I had checked out the Web site several times. *Just two hours east but several light-years away from New York City,* it boasted, *Le Refuge offers spiritual renewal in an atmosphere of unparalleled tranquility and serenity*. The photos showed a Belle Epoque mansion with outer buildings nestled in among the trees on untold acres of landscaped grounds. The promotional blurbs promised elaborate massage treatments, world-class yoga instructors, and an outdoor "serenity labyrinth" in which guests "walk the path to cosmic consciousness." There was also a list of stringent rules: *No pets. No alcohol. No food or beverages*

from the outside. Children under eighteen strictly forbidden. As I sali-
vated over the descriptions of four-handed Hawaiian Lomi-Lomi
massage treatments and fragrant body scrubs, Richard snidely re-
marked, "It's where the haute bourgeoisie acquires cultural capital
through conspicuous consumption." When he wants to, Richard
can suck all the joy out of life's oysters. A year ago, I liked to think
that our lives transcended crass materialism too. But now, I han-
kered for whatever could make my life more comfortable.

"Let's go this weekend!" Gigi shrieked. "I got nothing going on.
What about you girls?"

"Antonio and I are supposed to have lunch with his mother,"
Isla said. "But I am sure she would rather see him all by herself."

"I could use a break," Margaret chimed in. "I'll send Jonathan a
postcard, let him see what he's missing."

I had silently written off the possibility of joining them. Spiri-
tual renewal, I knew from Le Refuge's Web site, came at a hefty
material price: upward of $1,200 a night. Susan noticed my si-
lence. Then a look of awareness crossed her face. "Please come,"
she asked me. Then, she added, "I'm inviting you all as my guests!
I insist!"

I asked Susan about a dozen times if she was *sure* it was OK. Se-
cretly, I was thrilled. Then she got on her cell phone to make the
arrangements. Actually, she called her husband at the office and
spoke to his assistant, who made the arrangements, while Gigi,
Isla, and Margaret started chattering about what to pack. As
everybody else laughed raucously, I caught snatches of the con-
versation Susan was conducting into her phone. "No, just *three*
days." I heard a defensive note in her voice. "A long weekend *is*

a nice break," she said firmly. "Tell him it's all the break that I need." Then she asked, "May I speak to Harcourt?" Silence. "Oh. Well, please *tell* him that I called."

She put the phone away. I flashed on my run-in with Jessica in the park and her insinuations about Susan's marriage. But before I had a chance to say anything, Susan had joined in the conversation and the door to her private thoughts was firmly closed.

"But I was going to help you choose a stroller at Kmart on Saturday!"

I thought I detected a whiff of jealousy in Richard's voice that night. I had just told him of my swish weekend plans.

"We'll do it next Saturday," I said.

"I don't have time next weekend," he grumbled. "I have that deadline on the Wittgenstein paper, remember?"

"You can finish it while I'm gone," I countered. "You're always complaining you don't have enough time to write. Now you have a whole weekend free." Richard gazed at me with hurt, puppy-dog eyes. Then he nuzzled my belly. "I can't believe you want to go away without me," he mumbled. "I'll miss you."

"I'll miss you too," I smiled, already picturing myself floating in the spa's Olympic-sized pool, weightless and blissfully alone.

On Friday afternoon we piled ourselves into Margaret's and Susan's SUVs and our little convoy zoomed through the Midtown Tunnel and out of Manhattan. About two hours later, as we were entering the township of East Hampton, Gigi turned to Susan and said, "Why don't we swing by your place out here?" In fact, we were all eager to see Harcourt's fabled ancestral estate.

"Oh." Susan frowned. "Harcourt doesn't like it when I bring guests unannounced. He's kind of funny that way. He has an office there, and he's very particular about his space."

Gigi shrugged in disappointment.

Fifteen minutes later, we were settled in the Honeymoon Chalet of Le Refuge. The décor was a statement of expensive simplicity—clean-lined teak furniture, cream-colored silk upholstery, and soft, thick rugs. A capacious living room took up the front half of the house. Three bedrooms and three bathrooms filled in the rear. We oohed over the Frette linens and pillowy down comforters, the limestone fireplace, the pond-sized bathtubs, and the cavernous walk-in closets. I found an extra set of shampoo and body gel scented like fresh tangerines in one of the closets and quickly stashed them into my bag.

Susan seemed more at ease than I'd ever seen her. She opened the windows to let in the breeze, and the chalet smelled like sun and dandelions. We had put our suitcases in the same bedroom by tacit agreement. Gigi had volunteered to share a room with Margaret, and Isla took the smallest room by herself.

"Girls?" Susan called. "Let's eat!" She picked up the phone and I heard her order a round of fruit salads. "Can you throw a steak on top of that?" Gigi shouted from the other room. "I think," Susan answered with a laugh, "the three-bean burger is the closest thing they've got."

"Oh, for Christ's sake," Gigi grumbled. "I guess I'll have a couple of those."

Sheepishly, I asked if she wouldn't mind making it four. Isla and Margaret promptly made it eight three-bean burgers.

In the afternoon we set off on a stroll around the grounds. Large cypresses and oaks swayed in the breeze, spreading intricate, shifting shadows across the lush, broad lawn. Flowers blossomed in wild abundance, fountains tinkled, and Adirondack chairs beckoned from secluded corners. A handful of fellow guests padded around the grounds wordlessly in white terry-cloth robes. Aside from the rustling of the trees and the occasional chatter of birds, there was silence—the kind you forget even exists when you live in New York City.

As I strolled along the meandering pathways, my thoughts turned to Richard. I was certain that despite his condescending take on my getaway weekend, he would have reveled in these surroundings too. In my old days on the advertising agency payroll we'd been able to afford great vacations. We'd traveled to England, to Mexico, and of course, to Holland, on the trail of Richard's favorite seventeenth-century scholars—a trail that had led us to some strange places. "Spinoza lived here from 1661 to 1663!" he exclaimed as we drove up to an abandoned cottage in the middle of a suburban tract-housing development.

At the Spa Palazzo, a stand-alone building on the grounds that housed a pool, exercise classes, and treatment rooms, a pretty young assistant glanced at our bellies with poorly disguised alarm before handing us fluffy bathrobes and instructing us to leave our "civilian clothing" in lockers and head to the waiting room. There we were met by an officious older woman wearing a hospital-style outfit and holding a clipboard under her arm. "I hope you're enjoying your stay," the Spa Lady said, with the attitude of a stern nurse.

"Could you tell us what kinds of treatments you have?" I asked.

"We don't have 'treatments,'" Spa Lady corrected me. "We have wellness rituals."

"Do you have any 'rituals' to deal with *this?*" asked Gigi, pointing at her gargantuan belly.

The Spa Lady pursed her lips. "I'm afraid that we don't have any specific prenatal offerings," she said. "And we don't have prenatal bodywork tables, so you won't be able to get a massage. But perhaps you will find some of our other wellness rituals useful." She handed us a menu of services printed onto thick, papyrus-like paper. "Why don't you try the Banana Wrap-ture," she said. "That's our newest treatment."

I gathered that the treatment involved several different tropical oils, large green leaves, and mashed bananas. The printed description read like pornography for people who've given up on sex. I dithered, and then Susan made a suggestion. "You have to have the Shirodhara-Ayurvedic Fusion Journey," she said. "Trust me, you'll love it!"

So after Gigi went off for her Banana Wrap-ture, I told Spa Lady that I'd like "the Shirodhara Fusion thing," thinking that I was in for an hour of simple pleasures. My "Personal Healer" materialized and led me down a white carpeted hallway and into a small room. I sat on a reclining chair in the middle, facing a low table lined with jars of strange pastes. She scrutinized my face. "You have a *vata* personality but *kapha* skin," she announced loudly.

She shook her head as though I ought to have known better. Then she placed a large bowl full of a viscous, beige-colored substance in front of me and told me to put my feet in. The Journey, it turned out, began with an avocado and sesame-oil footbath and moved up to the head "chakra by chakra." I was assured I would arrive at the "zone of tranquility" by the end of the *two-hour* session, but only two minutes into the leg massage I entered the zone. When at last the therapist arrived at my head, she softly intoned, "Prepare for your inner journey." I closed my eyes obediently. She gave me a deft head massage. A few moments later, I felt a liquid pressure on my forehead. "I'm pouring sun-warmed oil onto your third eye," she said.

She might have been using Crisco, I was so happy.

On my way out, I felt as tender and well-seasoned as a spring lamb. I looked over the menu of "rituals" again and read the description of my particular treatment. My eye stopped on the word "Shirodhara."

Shirodhara . . . it sounded so exotic, so feminine.

What a wonderful name, I thought.

"You are all free spirits now," the yoga instructor told us later that afternoon, as we wrapped up the kind of lazy, slow-moving session to which only eight-months pregnant women are entitled. "Assume the position that comes to you spontaneously from within."

Margaret immediately launched herself in the Warrior One pose. Her arm stretched out like an arrow, and her pregnant belly was the bow.

Isla sat down and moved into the Lord of the Fishes pose. She twisted her legs in one direction and her upper body in the other. She was so flexible, you could never be sure which way she was facing.

Susan closed her eyes and clasped her hands together in the Mountain Prayer pose. She seemed to transport herself to some faraway glacial peak, accompanied only by the howling wind.

Gigi fell to her hands and knees, arched her back, screwed up her face, and hissed noisily. This was the Lion's Breath pose, the same one that had brought us all together in laughter only a few months previously.

And I, Laura, overwhelmed but happy for the moment, invented my own yoga move, which I dubbed the Flat on Your Back pose. It's where you lie down, watch your friends cope with the awesome prospect of motherhood, and surrender yourself to the mad rushing river that bears us all ceaselessly into the future.

"Wow, that was a great class!" Gigi enthused at the juice bar. "And that foot rub I had earlier . . ." She broke off and her expression turned sober.

"What?" I asked.

"John used to massage my feet when we were in bed," she said. "He really had the touch—nice and slow. Not like Milton. He never puts any muscle into it." She shook her head. "John was *bad*," she insisted, almost to herself. "Never saw a mirror he didn't like. But man, was he fun. . . ." She took a swig from a Detoxifying Rainforest Juice Blend served in an oversized wineglass. Gigi had

teetotaled her way through pregnancy, but, as she frequently re-
minded us, it hadn't been easy. "Thank God for my Milton. He
drives slow and he dresses like he's going to the library. God, I
love him."

When Gigi spoke about Milton, I could identify. Richard
lacked Milton's fancy pedigree, and I liked to think he was sex-
ier; still, they were both calm choices for excitable women.
One day over lunch, when Isla commented, "Sometimes I don't
know how I ended up with Antonio," Gigi and I had answered
simultaneously, "I know *exactly* why I married my husband!"
They were choices we had made with our heads, as well as our
hearts.

The other yoga mamas pulled up to the bar. Isla looked radi-
ant. Margaret seemed to have sweated out her worries. And Su-
san's blue eyes had a faraway look, as though she were nourishing
herself in the memory of some distant, happy time.

"Great place," Margaret said to no one in particular.

"I have some ideas about what I would do with it—if it were
mine, that is," Susan smiled.

"Yeah, like have a real bar," Gigi said.

"They could give us some real food too," said Isla, toying with
another three-bean burger.

"I was thinking of opening it to the whole family." Susan
laughed. "Start up prenatal classes and treatments, and get rid of
the no-children rule."

"You should buy this place," Gigi interjected. We all giggled at
her outrageous suggestion.

"I'm just hoping it's not overbooked for my ten-year

anniversary," Susan said. "Harcourt has promised that we'll celebrate it here, next April."

"Ain't he a sweetie," said Gigi.

We talked through the breezy summer evening. After sunset, we decided to go for a swim in the well-lit pool. I floated next to Susan for a while, and we reveled in the sudden weightlessness of our bellies as we watched the stars come out. "It must have been difficult to face the fertility treatments," I ventured, curious about her invisible husband. "Was Harcourt supportive?"

"He didn't like to talk about it. I guess they don't teach you how to talk about your feelings at the Saint Sebastian Academy. He's great with people in groups, but one-on-one is harder for him."

It was the first time I'd heard Susan even suggest a criticism of her husband. We paddled together in silence a while longer.

"One night, long before I got pregnant, I saw a little boy in a dream," Susan confided. "I was playing with him, singing to him. And suddenly I felt like I knew where I was going." Susan closed her eyes and entered the zone, effortlessly.

As I floated along in the warm water, I tried to imagine what life was like for my daughter in her liquid home. I felt her do one of her funny somersaults in my belly, then bump up against my abdomen wall, as if to reply, "I love it, Mom—I love you." "I love you too, sweetheart," I whispered back to her.

For a moment, I was about as close to heaven as you can get.

When I got back from Le Refuge the following night, I was still in the zone.

Richard looked half asleep on the couch, reading one of his obscure history books, but he roused himself when I came in. "I missed you, baby," he said. "I missed the both of you."

I said, "I think I know the name of our daughter."

He sat up. A faint look of alarm crossed his face. I hadn't actually made up my mind, but something about his look pushed me over the edge. "It's—it's Shirodhara!" I blurted.

Silence.

"Shirodhara!" I said, hearing a note of desperation in my voice. Richard just shook his head.

"Richard," I pleaded. "I'm carrying her. I'm her mother. This is a name I'll say a hundred times a day for the rest of my life. You get to give her your last name; can't I have the first?"

He gave me a cold look, then silently picked up his history book and resumed reading where he'd left off. A white-hot rage welled up from my core and the last ember of my glow from Le Refuge faded and died.

7

It is difficult to attain a human birth.

—SHARON GANNON AND DAVID LIFE, *JIVAMUKTI YOGA*

In the steamy heat of August, the yoga mamas ripened to the bursting point. I spent many days rarely moving more than a few feet from my welcoming bed, feeling my daughter squirming inside my belly and trying to guess which of her little limbs was bumping and pushing into my waiting hands. As we each approached our rendezvous with destiny, our different philosophies about the birthing process began to generate small sparks of friction. Susan kept suggesting that if your birth wasn't as natural as that of a cow in a meadow, you were cheating yourself of life's only truly authentic experience. Margaret took the view that if you failed to avail yourself of all the latest drugs and gadgets, you were shamelessly risking your child's health and your own. Isla tended to side with Susan, and Gigi usually backed up Margaret.

I couldn't make up my mind. So, as always when the stakes are high, I asked my mom.

"Richard and I are working on our birth plan," I said on one of our calls.

"Plan? But you're already pregnant, sweetie."

"I know, Mom. But all the other women are writing down how they want their delivery—"

"Laura, you can't plan a birth any more than you can plan the weather. It just happens. Like rain. All you have to do is make sure it happens in the *hospital*."

Susan was supposed to be the first of us to deliver, followed a few weeks later by Margaret. But Susan was two weeks overdue, which put them in a dead heat. The rest of us were starting to worry about Susan, but she was serene. "Gaia says it's perfectly natural," she told me, nodding her head, willing me to agree with her. In addition to hiring a midwife, Susan had asked Gaia to serve as her doula, or labor assistant. "She has me taking daily doses of primrose oil to ripen my cervix."

Susan lived in a duplex apartment in the heart of Soho. "We used to just have the bottom floor," she confided, "but one day Harcourt called the guy upstairs and asked if he wanted to sell it. Our neighbor said, 'Funny you should ask.'" Susan laughed. "I can barely keep up with Harcourt. That's what happens when you marry a man of ideas!"

As part of her birth plan, Susan installed a whirlpool bathtub the size of a small lake in her marble bathroom. She had also purchased a CD of a woman chanting in a strange monotone, while a gong sounded in the background. "I'm having a hypno-water-birth," she explained when she played it for us after class in the Hasharama studio. "Harcourt Jr. will move from water *inside* to water *outside* in a perfectly natural environment, and I'll have a pain-free delivery through self-hypnosis."

"Right," Margaret whispered. "And *my* baby is going to fly out of my head."

It made me a little nervous when Susan referred to her baby as "Harcourt Jr." Although she had submitted to an ultrasound, she had insisted she not be told her baby's sex. "I just know it's a boy," she said dreamily. Harcourt Sr., she added, really wanted a boy. The old Laura might have been tempted to raise the issue of female infanticide and skewed gender ratios in developing countries. But the new me just decided to change the subject.

"My water broke yesterday." It was Susan. She sounded incredibly calm. "Would you like to come over?"

I rushed to her apartment, and Gaia answered the door in an Indonesian-print smock, a large Native American pendant around her neck. In the living room, Susan was reclining on a leather club chair cradling a mug of foul-smelling tea. Her contractions, she reported, were irregular and far apart. The midwife was kneeling before Susan and massaging her bare feet. She was trying to locate the pressure point to induce labor, Susan explained. "Once they find that point, it's like an ejection button—whoosh!" she assured me.

Harcourt, as always, was not present.

"He's got some last-minute stuff at the office to take care of," Susan said. "He's been so good about calling. He's coming home soon."

"Drink up," said Gaia, nodding at her mug.

Susan took a sip, fighting back an expression of disgust. "The tea helps the contractions." She swallowed. "It's a technique women have been using since the Old Testament. All this ancient knowledge would be lost if not for people like Gaia."

Susan broke off as one of the contractions hit. She closed her eyes and was silent for about twenty seconds. Her focus turned entirely inward.

The phone rang. Susan motioned for me to pick it up.

"We're calling to check on her status," a woman said.

She sounded officious. "Who is this?" I asked.

"This is Mr. Fielding's personal assistant," the woman said brusquely.

"Everything seems fine, but perhaps you would like to speak with Susan," I said.

"Thank you, that won't be necessary," said the woman, and she hung up. I slowly replaced the telephone in its cradle.

"Was that Harcourt?" Susan asked hoarsely, her contraction abating.

"Yes," I replied. In her present condition she didn't need to know that Harcourt hadn't bothered to call himself.

Gaia looked at me and shrugged knowingly.

As morning turned to afternoon, Susan seemed to grow tired and distant, her contractions hitting at random intervals. I started to worry. I remembered from my prenatal classes that when your water breaks, you are supposed to go into the hospital within twenty-four hours. Otherwise, there is a risk of infection for both the baby and the mother. I walked into the hallway and tried to reach the others on my cell. Gigi was out, but Margaret was still in her office.

"I've got a client meeting in a couple minutes," Margaret snapped. "What is it?"

I told her about Susan's condition, how long it had been since her water broke, and she was livid. "Women can *die* in childbirth," she barked. "She needs a doctor."

"How are you feeling, by the way?" I asked.

"Not sure what's going on down there right now," Margaret said, as though irritated by the question.

I cornered Gaia and the midwife in the kitchen, where they were brewing another pot of her smelly tea. "Do you think Susan should go to the hospital?" I asked. "It's been a long time since—"

"Susan is progressing," the midwife cut me off.

I stared at them.

"I have a daughter too, you know," Gaia said, turning back to the tea. It was clear I was dismissed.

I returned to Susan. "Margaret and I are worried," I told her. "We think you should go to the hospital, just to be on the safe side."

"You called *Margaret?*" Susan's voice was faintly incredulous. I nodded.

"Margaret and I . . ." She raised her hands to demonstrate the world between them. "I *want* to stay at home," she continued firmly.

"Susan, we think that—"

"I just spoke with Harcourt and he agrees."

I doubted she had, but kept my face neutral.

"He says if I've gone this far, I shouldn't turn back now."

"Susan, I think maybe that's not such a good idea," I said.

"Well, I do," she snapped.

For the first time I heard her use the kind of steely tone ladies of the manor employ to dress down their domestics. It shocked me into momentary silence. I realized there was nothing more for me to do, so I wished Susan luck. I walked slowly back home through the hot August afternoon, nursing a dull pain inside and wondering if I knew Susan as well as I thought I did.

That evening, as Richard lay on the sofa reading one of Plato's dialogues, I paced our cramped apartment. Each time I tried to call Susan, her machine picked up.

"Stop worrying," Richard said. "Susan's probably had her baby already, and her astrologer is doing its chart right now."

But when the phone rang early the next morning, it was Margaret. "I think all that talk about Susan's labor got me going, if you know what I mean," she said.

"You're in labor?" I clutched the phone. "Congratulations!"

"It's nothing," she said calmly. "It's like having a big rubber band tightening around my belly. I feel great. Any word on Susan?"

"I haven't been able to get through," I said. "Shouldn't you be heading for the hospital?"

"Nah. All the textbooks say to wait until the contractions are closer together."

"Is there anything I can do?"

"Nah, my parents drove in from White Plains. I'm sitting here having a bagel and watching them fight with each other."

If Margaret was a perfectionist, I knew, it was because her parents lived in a state of permanent chaos. "I love them," she often told me. "But they are the most incompetent human beings I know." They were not taking her impending out-of-wedlock birth very well. "But where *is* the father?" they kept asking. They had long ago convinced themselves that Nick, her ex-law-school boyfriend of twelve years ago, was destined to be The One. For several years after the breakup, Margaret's mother continued to send him Brooks Brothers sweaters at Christmas. Nick was in fact Margaret's last— and really her only—serious boyfriend. "I've been doing eighty hours a week for ten years," she once said to me. "I don't even have time for houseplants. How am I supposed to have a love life?"

An hour later, Susan finally called. She sounded hysterical. Her labor had stalled overnight, then resumed fitfully in the morning. "I'm coming over!" I announced. Throwing on one of Richard's old T-shirts, I ran outside, hailed a taxi, and sped the few blocks down to Susan's building. I finally reached Gigi on my cell. She screeched, "We gotta get that girl to a fucking hospital! I'll call Isla!" and hung up.

The midwife answered the door with a worried expression.

Susan looked haggard, with dark circles under her eyes. "My cervix isn't dilating," she wailed. "The midwife tried to dilate me manually! It was the most painful thing I've ever felt!"

I buttonholed Gaia in the hallway, and she agreed that Susan should get to the hospital. "We're taking her in," I said to the midwife. She nodded grimly, and we went in to help get Susan dressed. "Where is your husband?" I asked.

"He already left for work." Her voice was practically a whisper.

"Give me his number," I demanded.

Harcourt's personal assistant answered the phone. "Mr. Fielding is busy right now," she said. "You can tell me what the problem is, and I will relay your message to him."

I yelled at her incoherently, there was a shuffle, then a man's voice barked, "What is it?" His voice sounded hard, not at all like the prince of the beach Susan had described. "I'm Laura, Susan's friend," I began.

"Oh," he said, in a way that made it sound like, "And?"

"Susan is in bad shape. She needs to get to the hospital—"

"Well, *Susan's friend,* my wife has a midwife taking care of her. I think she knows what she's—"

"*No,*" I interrupted. "Susan needs to get to the hospital, *now!*"

Silence.

"Damn it," I heard him say under his breath, "What a total fuckup." Then he started yelling at his assistant to reschedule some meetings. "I'll see her at the hospital," he said and slammed down the phone.

Gigi and Isla pulled up in Antonio's black Hummer. We all

bundled in. By now, Susan was beyond reason, alternately yelling and sobbing, then falling into intense silences. Isla drove to the downtown university medical center in the financial district, where the rest of us were planning to deliver. It was widely known as one of the best hospitals in Manhattan. It took us just ten eternal minutes to get there.

Gigi and I shouldered Susan into the lobby, while Gaia trailed behind and Isla parked the car. Susan's moans were getting louder and harsher.

"Let me call obstetrics," the intake nurse said. He mumbled on the phone, then looked up at us, "We have a bed for you."

A pair of paramedics appeared and loaded Susan into a wheelchair. Gaia took her pendant off her neck and placed it in her outstretched hand. "My work is done," she announced, giving Susan a final hug, then turning to leave. Gigi and I followed Susan to the elevator, shouting encouragements to her as the doors closed. Then we heard a bang and turned around to see Isla burst through the door of the hospital—with Margaret.

"Margaret? What are you doing here?" I asked.

Margaret looked at me incredulously. "Having my baby!"

"Aren't your parents here with you?" Gigi demanded.

"They're fighting in the car."

"What took you so long?" I asked, suddenly realizing that seven hours had passed since she had called to tell me that her contractions had started.

"Well, uh . . . you wouldn't believe . . . how long it takes my mother to pack ice cream and cookies. . . ."

She was obviously deep into her labor. The nurse shoved a

stack of insurance papers across the counter. Margaret took the forms and began to fill in the blanks methodically. Every minute or two her hand would freeze and she would let out an athletic grunt. Finally, she closed her eyes and put the papers down. I thought she was going say something to the nurse, but instead she turned and leaned against the wall.

"It broke," she stammered. "My water just broke!"

I noticed water running down her leg and pooling onto the floor.

The nurse got back onto his headset. "OK," he said, looking up at us. "You can take her up. Fifth floor, right and then right again out of the elevator. But I'm not saying they've got any rooms, your other friend took the last—"

We didn't hear the rest of it. Gigi and I took Margaret by the arms, while Isla waited behind for the fighting parents. "I think I'm ready for that epidural now," Margaret shouted.

Up in the obstetrics ward, a pair of nurses helped Margaret out of her clothes, into a gown, and onto a gurney. As we rolled down the hallway, looking for a place to park her, I heard moans and shrieks from every corner. One of the moans sounded familiar. I peeked inside a room, and sure enough, it was Susan.

"Park her here!" I said, pointing to the spot outside Susan's door.

"Hi, Suu-saahhn," Margaret gasped from her gurney.

"Oh, hi, Margaret?" I heard Susan say, breathlessly.

A cheerful, middle-aged Asian man approached Margaret. "Now, let's see," he said, tapping Margaret playfully on the knee.

"I'm Dr. Suh, and I'm here to give you an epidural, right? Your name is Mrs. Susan Fielding?"

"He's mine!" Susan screamed. *"In here! In here!"*

"Don't even think about it, sister!" Margaret yelled. She reached for the doctor's arm and yanked him to her side. *"She* is having a *natural* birth! Shoot *me* up, *now!"*

"I'm Susan, Dr. Suh!" Susan whimpered.

"I'm Susan Fielding!" Margaret screamed.

The anesthesiologist looked at Margaret. "You're not Mrs. Fielding, are you?"

"I am!"

He looked at me. I shook my head.

"Let's get someone to look at you while I deal with Mrs. Fielding," he said. He waved toward a nurse as he slipped into Susan's room and shut the door behind him. One of the nurses came over to examine Margaret. "Wow, you're fully dilated!" she said, sounding genuinely surprised. *"Where's Dr. Suh?!"* Margaret screamed.

"No time for that, honey," the nurse said. "You're ready to go!" The nurse began to wheel Margaret away. "And who are you?" she asked, turning to us.

"Uh, friends?"

"You'll have to leave. Only family at this point," she said, nodding to the direction of the exit. "Unless you want to stick around for your own deliveries." She laughed as she waved her clipboard in the direction of our bellies.

We retreated quietly to the hospital lobby, stunned.

After we found Isla and filled her in, we sat in silence for a while. Then Gigi said, "Come on, girls. Let's go visit Milton. He'll take us out for something to eat." Milton worked only a few blocks away, in the heart of the financial district. She dialed him on her cell phone, and we agreed to meet him at his office and go out for a quick bite.

Milton's firm occupied the same building as the Morgan Sachs investment bank, which had been his employer before he started his own firm. With its lobby of marble and mirrors and the bustle of men and women in tailored business suits, you could almost smell the money. We were headed toward the bank of elevators when Gigi suddenly ducked behind a nearby pillar and turned to face the wall. She was shaking.

"What is it?" I asked with alarm, thinking it was her turn to "pop."

"It's *John*," she whispered. Out of the corner of my eye, I saw the figure of a tall, well-built man with curly dark hair, marching on an inevitable collision course with us.

"Don't look! He can't see me pregnant!" she screeched in my ear.

I glanced at Isla. She had continued on ahead and was stuck out in the open, in between John and us. I knew she had heard Gigi. Luckily, Isla knew exactly what to do. She dropped her purse, allowing its contents to spill on to the floor. Of course, John stopped to help her. "You just relax," he said gallantly, bending down to pick up her things. "And congratulations, by the way."

"That is so kind of you," Isla murmured.

Gigi gave me a look somewhere between panic and incomprehension.

"Your husband is a lucky man," I heard John say.

"Hah, what husband?" Isla grumbled, as if in a private comment to herself.

"You know," he said, "nothing makes a woman more beautiful than impending motherhood." He stooped down to pick something off the ground. "This must be yours," he said, scooping up one of the calling cards Isla carried. "What a remarkable card—and what a remarkable name—Isla."

I could hardly believe what I was hearing. Was John flirting with an eight-months-pregnant woman? Yes, he was! Gigi shot me a knowing grimace to confirm, yes, that's John all right.

I could see that Isla was looking forward to blowing him off. Just as she moved to retrieve her card, however, she sensed that he was about to turn around and face us. "Oh, please, *take* my card," she said strategically. "You might need it sometime."

"My name is John." He smiled. Isla held his gaze just long enough for Gigi and me to turn the corner into the safety of the elevator bank. Giving John a friendly good-bye, Isla joined us.

Gigi looked at me and then at Isla. Then she looked back at me. I wilted. "Gigi, I . . . I accidentally—"

"Laura did not mean to tell me," Isla interrupted. "I pulled it out of her."

"I'm sorry, Gigi," I said.

"Nobody else knows about him," Isla continued. "*Nobody* else."

Gigi seemed to make up her mind. "Laura, if you hadn't told Isla, we'd never have made it past him," she said with finality. "This is the way it had to be. Jeez, I'm swimming in my own can of worms. But what a sleaze! Did you *see* how he—"

"Darling!" Milton popped out of one of the elevators. With his high forehead and earnest expression, he had the look of a man who has no idea just how bad other people can be. His smile changed to alarm, however, when he saw his flustered wife. "Are you OK?"

"It's . . . it's just . . ." Gigi stammered, her eyes turning teary.

"Don't worry, I'm sure Susan and Margaret are in good hands," he crooned. As tears started to spill down Gigi's cheeks, Milton enveloped her in a reassuring bear hug and added, "Everything will be all right."

Gigi squeezed Milton back and mustered a weak smile, raising her eyebrows at Isla and myself over his shoulder.

8

Yoga is what happens to you, not what you want to happen.

—SUSAN FIELDING, YOGA MAMA

Two days later, Gigi, Isla, and I streamed into Margaret's hospital room, trailing a cloud of balloons and bouquets. She looked pale, but otherwise composed. She wore a pretty white dressing gown, obviously selected for the occasion. Her short nails were perfectly painted a delicate shade of blush.

"I am so *proud* of you!" Gigi said. We all hugged Margaret as best we could. Her cell phone buzzed and broke up our moment.

"Hi, Mom. We're great. Tell Dad pepperoni's fine." And then, switching to another caller: "Nah, let's skip the letter before action. Just serve the bastard."

To her side, in a small plastic crib, swaddled in hospital white and green, lay the real object of my interest: a luminous baby boy, dozing off in a well-earned sleep. Nathan weighed in at a healthy seven pounds seven ounces. I tried to wrap my mind around the fact that this perfect baby had been living inside Margaret's petite body just a short while ago. We cooed over her baby's impossibly tiny features. He seemed so sweet-natured, so strangely beautiful with his pale moon face. I patted my own belly absently, astonished that a living being like the one in front of me was squirming away inside my own belly. *Will she be as perfect? Are all her limbs in the right places? Will she have too many toes and not enough brain cells?* Nate gave a happy yawn and I relaxed. My daughter would turn out just fine.

Gigi inquired gingerly, "Any word from the father? I bet he'll be proud."

"I've served him," Margaret replied.

We looked at each other perplexed.

"What did you serve to him?" Isla asked.

"A paternity suit," Margaret explained. "I've served him with a paternity suit."

"So I guess he'll find out about Nate now," I volunteered, uncertainly.

"Yeah," said Margaret softly, and for a moment, as she gazed at the sleeping angel by her side, I thought I caught a look of sorrow on her face. Then her voice grew steely. "He'll find out—and so will everyone in his office. I'm having them track him down and serve the papers in his office in the middle of the day. I want to make sure all his secretaries and associates see it."

I watched Nate's tiny chest rise and fall and wondered how it could be that there was a man out there who didn't know or care that this boy was his. After more heartfelt cooing and solicitousness, we shuffled across the hall, trailing a few more balloons and a special-order organically farmed bouquet. Susan gave us a wan smile as she cuddled her sleeping newborn. Harcourt, naturally, was nowhere to be found. He apparently made it in time to see the baby, but then returned to work.

"I am so happy," Susan said softly. She shifted uncomfortably in her bed.

"Does it hurt a lot?" I asked.

"I feel wonderful," she said. But I knew that the fresh stitches on her lower abdomen would take time to heal. Susan had started her labor like a cow in the meadows of Soho, but the three-day ordeal led to complications and, ultimately, a cesarean-section birth.

"Any sign of Gaia?" Gigi asked abruptly.

"Oh, yes, she sent me a beautiful baby sling," Susan said serenely. Then, catching our reproachful stares, she added, "They did their best. It's not Gaia's fault. Yoga is what happens to you, not what you want to happen."

Her blissful tone relieved my concern about the one other "complication" of her birth: Harcourt Jr. turned out to be a beautiful, seven-pound baby *girl*.

To the surprise of the yoga mamas, Susan didn't seem to mind at all. In fact, she behaved as if she had been expecting a girl all along, calling the baby by name, Honor, as though we had been long familiar with it. I wondered how Harcourt felt about the matter, but I thought the better of asking.

The rest of the yoga mamas dropped like tomatoes off the vine. Isla, like Susan, had chosen to use a midwife, but in her case the midwife practiced within a special wing of the hospital and safely guided her through seven hours of uncomplicated labor. She was rewarded with a baby girl who could not have looked more like her father. They named her Azula.

"I had a dream," Gigi told me in one of our daily phone conversations. "I was in the delivery room and the baby came out, and everybody was fussing over him. Then I stood up and yelled, 'Hey! Can I get a glass of merlot?'"

I knew Gigi's number was up when the phone didn't ring for a whole day. Early the next morning she called.

"Whoa, sugar pie, was that something!" she exclaimed. "My little Charles came out like a bombshell. Nine pounds two ounces! I knew this one was going to be a handful. He's got a bad attitude. Just like his mama!"

"Who does he loo——" I started to say, and then cut myself off. *Damn it,* I thought, *how could I be so stupid?*

Gigi knew exactly what I meant to ask. "I don't know," she said. "I mean, he looks just like me. Or like what I'm *gonna* look like when I'm an *old man*." There was silence on the line, then she added hopefully, "I think he's got Milton's eyes." She sighed. "But Milton's mother was here this morning, and do you know what she said? She said, 'He doesn't have the Chad-worth chin.' "

"Relatives *always* make that kind of comment," I reassured her. "The baby comes out and suddenly everybody is analyzing the eyebrows and the nose and the fingers like they're pieces of a jig-saw puzzle."

"I know, sweet pea, I know," Gigi said. "That's just who she is. A Miss Know-It-All, a real Buttinsky. But hey, she's seventy-six. So she's headed in the right direction. Know what I'm saying?"

I smiled, in spite of myself, on the other end of the line.

"So listen, mama," Gigi said cheerfully, "looks like you're next!

It was 10 P.M. when I finally felt the dull pains begin. "This is not so bad!" I said to Mom on the phone.

"Honey, I think it's time for you to get to the hospital."

"I don't want to go to the hospital. I want to go to Le Refuge!" I giggled. "I'll give birth in the swimming pool!"

"Put Richard on, please."

Richard took my arm nervously and led me downstairs. We hailed a taxi out of the warm night and sped off.

"Dumb fuck!" Richard yelled as another cab cut us off.

We entered the obstetrics ward and were installed in a room with enough medical equipment to build a robot. The "homey" pink flowers stenciled above the windows seemed a little desper-ate. But the contractions were now so intense that I soon lost track of the outside world. I focused all my energy on the invisi-ble pain point that seemed to lie somewhere deep inside of me.

Then Richard grabbed me and tried to hold me as if we were dance partners.

"What the hell are you doing?" I yelled, pushing him away.

"I read about this in the birthing book. It's the Last Tango method. Dancing and breathing to ease labor pains."

I looked at him in horror. "You fucking alien!" I screamed. "Sit down!! Don't move! And don't talk!"

After the drugs kicked in, I relaxed for several hours. I even slept for a time. When I awoke, I could feel my baby girl moving up and down inside of me, as though she were using my diaphragm as a springboard.

The doctor came in and put herself into position.

Richard and the nurses started to chant encouragements.

I asked them to put a mirror in place, so that I could see the action. "There's plenty of room down there!" I bellowed. Then I asked them to remove the mirror. It was all getting too graphic. *Way too graphic.* Every thirty seconds, in time with some fierce contractions, I pushed as hard as I could. Richard kept up his rah-rah chants, but I could tell from his face that he was seeing some shocking things. Then, with a final, eyeball-splitting push, my baby came out in one great whoosh.

Just like in the movies, she let out a lusty cry.

And, just like in the movies, it was the sweetest sound I'd ever heard.

I pleaded with everyone to bring her to me right away. A minute or two later, after she'd been cleaned and weighed, the doctor placed her on my chest. Like a little animal, she scrabbled up my breast and started sucking. I could see that she knew more about our new situation than I did. I'd worried that I didn't know anything about how to be somebody's mom. But right then, I realized that she would teach me whatever it was that I needed to know.

As I lay with my baby in the recovery ward, a nurse approached us with the paperwork. The moment for naming our baby had come, and we still hadn't resolved the issue. Richard lifted up the paper gingerly.

"Anna?" he said, in a tentative voice.

Anna, I thought, in a blissful stupor. She could be named "Brunhilde" and she'd still be the love of my life. "Anna, how sweet," I said as I cradled my precious child in my arms.

And that was all it took. Richard scribbled in the forms and ran off to turn them in before I could say anything more.

9

The yogi should be freed from household worries.
He [sic] should therefore preferably beg his food, but
he must be very cautious that this food is pure
and conforms with the rules of yoga.

—ALAIN DANIÉLOU, *YOGA: MASTERING THE SECRETS OF MATTER AND THE UNIVERSE*

I had not anticipated how much I would love my daughter on
sight. The first few nights after her birth, Richard and I stayed
awake just watching her sleep and marveling at our luck. "I never
knew I could love anything so much!" I told Gigi when she called
to congratulate us. "It's as though my heart instantly doubled in
size!" Unfortunately, my sleep cycle was cut in half, then quar-
tered, and finally scattered like precious dust along an unending
highway of days and nights. My first attempts at breast-feeding
were excruciating.

"My boobs are hard as rocks," I confessed to Susan over the

telephone. "I feel like a pair of zeppelins just landed on my chest."

"Try using cabbage leaves as a compress," she suggested.

Richard sneered that Susan was hardly one to give advice, but I stuffed my bra with cabbage leaves anyway. I looked like an incompetent shoplifter at a Midtown deli, but it seemed to work. My milk started flowing and the zeppelins deflated. Just in time, as now Anna demanded to be fed every few minutes throughout the day and night, which made it impossible to do anything other than sit half naked with her on the couch.

Our apartment was a mess, with overflowing garbage bins, dirty dishes piled on the kitchen table, and clothes and newspapers strewn all over the floor. Then the grandmothers descended. First Richard's mother arrived, with plenty of unsolicited advice: "Don't let her spend more than five minutes at each breast," "Just let her sleep through the night," and my personal favorite, "Let her cry, it's good for her lungs." I could hardly hide my relief when rumors of an outbreak of mad cow disease forced her to return to her farm in Montana.

My mom was equally merciless. She flew in from San Diego a few days after birth, picked her way around our tiny, littered apartment, and shook her head. *New York,* she said. "I just don't get it." She headed for our 1940s-era kitchenette and immediately began to make lasagna. In Mom's world, there is no problem that can't be solved with a good casserole. "We need to have a little more order here," she said, as she sliced the cheese that appeared mysteriously out of her bag.

"Mom, I just had a *baby!*" I said.

"That's exactly the point."

"That's what I keep saying," Richard chimed in. Richard seemed to think that the answer to all our problems was to teach Anna the concept of time. He thought that getting her to eat and sleep on schedule would be no more challenging than getting undergraduates to show up promptly for their lectures.

Anna started screeching maniacally for milk. "Try scheduling this!" I retorted. I eased back into bed with her, propping myself up on my elbow and dangling my breast. She latched on ferociously.

"That's an unusual way to breast-feed," Mom said.

"It works."

"You've always been so *creative,* Laura." In momspeak, "creative" was a code word for "incomprehensible."

I rolled over in the bed and landed on half a cinnamon Danish on a plate. I peeled off the Danish and lay back on a feast of muffin crumbs stored under one of the pillows. Richard always left his dirty dishes exactly where they were when he finished his meals, which in this case was beside the bed. "Leave them exactly where you last used them," he once explained his "dish theory" to me. "Then, when there are no more clean dishes, organize a massive clean-up, late at night, when you're not good for doing anything else. It's a much more efficient use of time."

The truth was, Richard simply regarded the physical details of life as inessential. The way he floated above the concerns of the material world had been so appealing to me when we met. Let *mundane* people worry about the organization of worldly tasks,

I thought. Eventually, Richard will reveal the mysteries of the Counter-Reformation to the masses. Now I thought that life on the higher plane was just squalid.

"He's a slob!" I complained to Mom.

As the warm smell of lasagna filled the room, I paced back and forth in the apartment trying to lull Anna into sleep. She waved her tiny arms and whimpered, tired but unable to let go. I tried singing. For no very good reason, the words to "Goodbye Yellow Brick Road" came to me, even though in our cramped studio we were very far from where the howling old owl in the wood would ever hunt the horny black toad.

I looked at Richard for help. He took her from my arms, and she wailed louder. Then he climbed onto the bed and stood up, holding Anna in his arms, and bounced up and down, using the natural springiness of the mattress to rock her. "What the *hell* are you *doing?*" I yelped. "It's more efficient this way," he explained, breathlessly. "I'm getting some good bouncing motion here with minimal effort. She likes it." I snatched my baby from her demented father.

To my disbelief, Mom seemed to think that Richard was making a decent show as a new father. "What, are you kidding?" I fumed. She gave me an odd look. "Dad didn't pick you up until you could crawl," she said. We caught each other's eyes, and in a momentary flicker, the thought passed between us. *If only Dad could have been here with us to see his first grandchild.*

Mom eventually succeeded where Richard and I failed. She scooped Anna from my arms and, with funny cackling noises, finally persuaded the little one to close her eyes. "How did you raise *three* of us?" I whispered to her as we tiptoed away from the crib.

"It was easy. I just locked two of you in the closet." She smiled.

"Milton's in the doghouse," Gigi said over the phone. "He thinks his job ends with handing out cigars."

"Antonio, he is a dog too!" Isla said when I called her. "He says he must wash his hands every time he touches Azula! So he never touches her! And I have not showered myself in three days!"

Margaret was bittersweet. She loved her Nate fiercely, and part of her didn't want maternity leave to end. "But I've never been away from the office for so long," she said. I heard a frown in her voice.

Only Susan seemed to greet motherhood with unalloyed pleasure. "Honor is an old soul," she whispered. "And breast-feeding is such a transcendental experience."

I needed my yoga mamas. I needed their absolute *empathy*. Not advice, not criticism; just a simple "I know!" And yet, there was a difference between them and me. They had cleaning ladies. And all but Susan had hired baby nurses to help them through the first months of infancy. It came down to this: The nannies made it possible for the other mamas to sleep. As little sleep as fussy Anna was getting, I was getting even less. After my mom ended her two-week mission of mercy, I stopped sleeping altogether. Pretty soon I had the hollow-eyed look of a screaming figure in an Edvard Munch painting. Now, if my thoughts turned to that TV ad for the Cheetah, I pictured a baby screaming in the background as the young man roars off in his driving machine. *Stop the noise . . . lose the baggage*.

Which reminded me, Robin had never called me back about that campaign.

When Anna was four weeks old, Robin finally took my call. "Hey, I want to meet the baby!" she gushed, after I bulldozed my way through the administrative assistants to get to her. She suggested visiting me at home, but I proposed we meet at a trendy restaurant instead. After endless days indoors with Anna, I was desperate to dress up like my old self again and see the world.

On the appointed day, I squeezed into a skirt and twinset, wrapped my hair into a neat bun, and dusted off a pair of Jimmy Choos that I held on reserve for client meetings. I dabbed some foundation under my eyes, hoping to disguise the dark circles that had taken up residence. Then I saddled Anna up in my BabyBjörn, carefully adjusting the resulting creases on my sweaters. I had come to love my Björn. It kept Anna close to my breast. And it solved my stroller problem for the time being. We didn't have the money for a Frog, I knew; but I wasn't ready for Kmart, either.

Robin showed up in jeans. She immediately lunged for Anna, cooing in a loud voice. Then she assaulted me with questions about Anna's sleeping schedule and eating habits. For the past five years, she and her husband had been debating the pros and cons of reproduction. Neither one could make up their mind.

"I think women just have to choose," she said, looking at me meaningfully.

I insisted that newborn babies were just like new handbags—impressive-looking accessories, but requiring minimal care, leaving their mothers with *plenty* of time and energy to write witty advertising campaigns. But Anna seemed to have an instinctive grasp of the issues at stake and did her best to thwart my efforts at putting my professional life back on track. Every time I got Robin near the subject of Amalgamated Motors or other, possible assignments, Anna gurgled or burped or wailed for my attention, bringing the conversation right back to the topic of reproduction. When I got home, with Robin's tinny coos and congratulations still ringing in my ears, I realized that she had not said a single word about my job prospects.

When Richard got home that evening, I was still wearing the skirt and twinset.

"Fancy!" He wiggled his eyebrows.

I scowled and told him the story of my meeting with Robin. "So much for 'freelancing,'" I concluded bitterly.

"So cultivate new clients," he answered.

"With what free time?" I replied. "Anna's a twenty-four-hour job, in case you haven't noticed. Besides, people are already forgetting about me. By the time I can work again, they'll be like, 'Laura who?'"

I was hoping for sympathy. But Richard's retort was defensive. "Hey, it's not like I have it so easy," he said. "My career's taking a hit too." He could flee to the library during the day, he admitted, but at night there was no respite from the demands of our creature.

This infuriated me.

"So what if you lose a little sleep here and there?" I yelled.

"*I'm* the one staying up all night with Anna, not you. *I'm* the one on the front lines of this battle. And I'm the one who's going to come out of it qualified for *nothing but a minimum-wage job!*"

I scooped up Anna, took her into the bedroom, and slammed the door behind me. I sat on the bed, trembling with frustration. It wasn't Richard's fault that Robin seemed to have given up on me professionally. But still, I couldn't help but think he was getting a free ride.

Most of my old friends were no more understanding than Richard.

I had always heard the story told from the other end: how, after having a baby, so-and-so lost all interest in her social circle, became a "baby bore," and retreated to the suburbs. But the other side of the story, I now realized, was that people without kids just didn't understand. I heard from my hard-partying PR friend at 11 P.M. one night. Her call roused me from a hard-won thirty minutes of sleep.

"Hey, Laura, congrats on the baby! Wow! You did it!" she was shouting into her cell phone. In the background I heard loud conversation and glasses clinking. "I'm at a great party in your neighborhood," she continued. "Why don't you join us?"

I wanted to reach down the phone line and whack her over her head. How could she call a house with a newborn baby so late?

By the time Anna was six weeks old, I could wait no longer. I had to see my yoga mamas. So far, telephone contact had been enough. Now it was time to regroup.

10

Blessed are the flexible
For they shall not be bent out of shape.

—ANONYMOUS

Everywhere you look in New York you see billboards flashing breasts in the name of everything from lingerie to mineral water. You never see advertisements showing them doing what they were made for. I never noticed this paradox in marketing until the yoga mamas, together with the yoga babies, met for our first autumn lunch at the Healthy Harvest.

We had just begun to chomp through our supersized portions of salad when Isla's daughter started to whine with hunger. Positioning Azula across her lap, Isla pulled up her navy cashmere sweater and offered her a breast. Azula latched on with single-minded ferocity. After a few minutes, Isla started to look uneasy and tried to drape her sweater over her infant. Azula wasn't having any of it; she batted the sweater away.

"What are you doing?" Gigi asked.

Isla nodded toward a nearby table. "They are showing me the evil eye."

We all looked over. Two conservatively dressed older women were clucking with disapproval at Isla's bared nipple. Gigi's eyes narrowed. Suddenly, she jerked her own sweater back and lifted up her shirt to reveal a full, baby-ready bosom. "I think Charles is *hungry,*" she announced, loud enough for the other women to hear. *Why not?* I thought. With a single, practiced motion, I, too, flipped my shirt and bra out of the way and exposed my nipple to strangers for the first time in my life. Anna burbled with delight. Susan and Margaret joined the crowd.

Faced with such a display of militant breast-feeding, our antagonists had little choice but to reposition their chairs in the opposite direction. It was our right to use our breasts to do what they were made for, wherever and whenever the need arose. We were feeding our infant children. Anyone who had a problem with that could just look away.

While we had been busy giving birth, the management of Hasharama had decided to go mainstream. They hired a chirpy instructor to run a practical, fitness-oriented class for new mothers: Mommy & Me Yoga. Gigi, Margaret, and I loved it. "Who needs all that *woo-woo?*" Gigi said.

Gaia was not happy. "The administration of Hasharama is full of charismatic personalities, but they appear to have become distorted by Anger and Ego," she announced in a circular to her pupils. "Even yoga practice can perpetuate bondage if the underlying intention is to serve the small self, not the Higher Self." She set up her own yoga studio across the street. Hasharama fired back with a seminar on "Healing the Angry Disciple." Isla, who was the most physically gifted among us, followed Gaia. And Susan, amazingly, remained loyal to her former doula.

The yoga mamas were now split between rival yoga camps.

Gigi wasn't long for breast-feeding.

At a subsequent lunch at Healthy Harvest, she raised a glass of wine and said, "Well, girls, here goes—my first drink since I found out I was pregnant." She took a very long sip, then exhaled loudly. "Ahhh, that's more like it!" She turned—wineglass in hand—to play with little Charles, who was dressed as always in a Ralph Lauren sweater, tiny golf pants, and infant-sized Top-Siders. He looked at her with a startled expression as if to say, "You're my *mother?!*"

Gigi looked back at him with equal surprise. "Can you believe I've got an accent like this, and my baby's in the *Social Register*?" she asked proudly. I could see that she was scrutinizing Charles's face. She caught my eye. "Now that I've had a drink," she said, whispering into my ear, "I think he looks like my Milton."

Every lunch after that, Gigi had a glass of merlot in hand and Charles had a bottle of formula.

* * *

While the rest of us lingered over our lunches that fall, Margaret often zoomed in and out of the Healthy Harvest like a boomerang. She always wore business attire and what I like to call "bitch shoes": pointy-toed slingbacks or low-heeled spectator pumps, stylish yet uptight. "Doesn't anyone realize that it's fucking impossible to work a real job, take care of a baby, and look presentable at the same time?" she asked me as she sat down one day for dessert.

Margaret needed the yoga mamas as much as I did. But there was no denying that her situation was different. When Susan or Gigi would compare notes on Soho's beauty salons and day spas, Margaret would turn to me and say dismissively, "God, who has the time?" She knew that even if I *did* have the time to pursue the same leisure activities as the other mamas, I didn't have the money. And she knew there had once been a time when I, too, had a career—*a very long time ago,* I thought bitterly.

Margaret's resentment about her work situation was nothing compared to the head of steam she was building up around the figure of Jonathan—Nate's "deadbeat dad." In the course of their epic legal struggle, Margaret and Jonathan had agreed to a temporary arrangement whereby he would take the baby for one day and one night twice a week. Jonathan, as far as I could tell, never missed a date with his son. Margaret was convinced that his paternal affection was a sinister ruse, a bald attempt to improve his prospects for a favorable judgment from the court.

"He shows up now," she said. "But I'm sure he'll eventually

disappear from Nate's life. He is pure evil. I'm going to see if I can have him disbarred."

Jessica, the designer blond from our original yoga class, also liked to meet friends at Healthy Harvest after class because, as she said, "The food here helps me stick to my diet." She had given birth to Cameron in the same week Anna was born.

Jessica always made an entrance. Her outfits were up-to-the-minute and perfectly accessorized. With her blond ringlets and wide-set eyes, she favored the kind of pale clothing that keeps dry-cleaners in business. I hadn't looked so spotless since before I got pregnant. Jessica's secret was simple. Unlike the rest of us, she never brought her baby to lunch. In fact, as far as I could tell, she never brought her baby anywhere. I'd seen her a half dozen times since her son's birth, but I'd never seen Cameron. "Our nanny is so attached to him, she'd feel left out if I took him away from her," she once told me.

One afternoon, she spotted our group. Arranging a smile on her face, she planted herself in front of Susan. "Wow!" she said, squinting at a pair of antique diamond drops that dangled from Susan's lobes. "Those look heavy!"

Jessica faked her jealousy so well I was pretty sure it was real.

"Thank you," Susan replied. "Actually, my husband's mother asked me to wear them when we got married. They've been in her family for years."

"Nice mother-in-law," Jessica said appreciatively. "Great gift."

Susan smiled uneasily. "Oh, well, they're not really mine."

"Are they part of the prenup?" said Jessica, picking up on Susan's discomfort.

I sputtered into my carrot juice. Not counting tabloid personalities, I'd never known any women who had prenups. Jessica brought it up as casually as if she were discussing car insurance. Susan looked embarrassed. "Oh, it's no big deal." Jessica laughed. "I have a prenup myself!"

I thought about Richard and wondered what our prenuptial agreement would have looked like. "If you leave, I get the CD collection." "If I leave, you get a share of my freelance income or ten dollars, whichever is greater."

Gigi frowned. "If my Milton ever tried to give me a prenup, I'd nix that idea right in the bag. I don't believe in prenups; they're for cheaters."

Susan quickly agreed with her. "I didn't really want one. But our lawyer—I mean, Harcourt's lawyer—seemed to think it was a good idea." She shrugged her shoulders, and the diamond earrings sparkled. "I really don't think it matters."

"Of course it doesn't," Jessica broke in, sounding slightly disingenuous. She turned to Gigi. "I'm sure Susan has a consent clause and a cheater clause."

Susan shifted uncomfortably.

"What clauses?" Gigi asked, perplexed.

"A consent clause basically says that if he up and leaves without your consent, and you're still meeting all your wifely obligations, you get to keep the money," Jessica explained. "And the cheater clause means that if either one of you cheats, the other can leave and keep the money. Standard stuff."

"You're covered, aren't you?" Gigi asked Susan with raised eyebrows.

"Oh, yes," Susan said, a little flustered. "We did that. I guess if Harcourt ever leaves me I'll be rich." She shrugged her shoulders, as if the idea that Harcourt would ever leave her, let alone cheat on her, was beyond the realm of possibilities.

"But what happens if you ever leave him?" Jessica persisted.

"Oh, well, in that case I'd be out on the streets!" she said with a nervous laugh. "But why would I ever want to leave Harcourt?"

"How long have you and Harcourt been married?" Jessica asked.

"We're coming up on our ten-year anniversary. This April. We're going to celebrate it at Le Refuge, where we had our wedding!" Susan smiled brightly, clearly hoping she had changed the subject.

"I hear that place is amazing!" Jessica exclaimed. "Our anniversary is in April too! Of course, it's only our third. We haven't figured out how to celebrate yet."

"Harcourt has been working on the details for us," Susan said, almost apologetically. "I don't know how he does it. He's got so much stuff going on at once, between work and . . ." Her voice trailed off. She looked lost.

"Oh, I'm sure he's very busy," Jessica said. She let slip a small smirk. "Well, I've gotta run!" she added. "Looks like my lunch dates have arrived." She headed off to join several well-dressed women at a table on the other side of the room.

"Harcourt really is sweet," Susan said to me a little defensively. "He says he wants to arrange for me to see a therapist to help me cope with my new circumstances. He says motherhood is too challenging to face alone."

"Motherhood is too challenging to face alone?" Isla mocked Susan's whispery voice with a sneer. We often lingered after lunch over herbal tea, after the other mamas had left. "Who will face motherhood for her? A man?" She looked at me incredulously.

I shook my head, and told her I had no idea, but it certainly wouldn't be a man. "Men," Isla snorted. "All Antonio cares about me now is my weight. 'When are you going to lose the pregnancy pounds?' he says to me! He is as bad like my agent!"

I whined about Richard, as I usually did when Isla brought up the subject of Antonio. "There is nothing I detest more than the sight of Richard reading the newspaper!" I said, and Isla nodded knowingly. I'd be ragged after yet another long night of heavily interrupted sleep. I'd have changed the baby twice, fed her a half dozen times, unloaded and reloaded the dishwasher, taken out the garbage, swept the floor. I'd greet my husband when he shuffled into the kitchen in the morning, thinking he'd give me a break. Instead, he'd head over to the couch with his coffee, flop down, and bury himself in the morning paper. "Do you know the last time I got to read the paper?" I would scream. Then he'd fold up the paper quietly and hand it to me, which only made me madder.

Isla gritted her teeth. "Do you know what Antonio wants to buy for himself now? He wants to buy a sport car, you know, a convertible! You cannot even fit a baby into that car! I say to him, if you are going to have a midlife crisis, please don't be like the typical middle-aged guy in some stupid novel!"

I stirred my herbal tea furiously, thinking about my failed advertising campaign for the Cheetah. I now had Robin pegged up with Richard and Antonio on the dartboard of my mind.

Isla shook her head with disgust. "He is going to the gym every day to give himself the right image for his restaurant. I think he just wants to be the superstar again, with all of the young girls giving him so much attention!"

Suddenly she looked afraid. "I think I know the one he has his eye on. Son of a mongrel dog!"

I was too frazzled to take on Isla's jealousies. So I sipped my tea in silence.

"Laura, do you remember that guy Gigi used to go with?" she said after a long pause.

I nodded. Of course, Gigi's John.

"He called me last night."

I nearly spat out my tea. "Did you speak to him?"

"Well, I told him that I was very busy, but . . ."

"But what?"

"Well, we did talk." Her face lit up. "Actually, for a long time."

I was stunned. For a moment, I felt a giddy sense of triumph. Motherhood was no exemption from the laws of attraction! But quickly my thoughts were overtaken with another concern. "Isla! What about Gigi?"

"I know, it is complicated," she conceded. "But I don't think that he did anything wrong to her. They were going together, and she told him that it was finished. It was her decision."

I had to agree.

"When I talked to John, he is actually very sympathetic. I told him about Antonio."

"You did?" It was one thing for Isla to complain to me. It was another for her to seek sympathy from a stranger. I knew Isla was looking for my understanding, but all I felt was vicarious guilt. "So what did he say?"

"He says that he wants to have his own child someday. He says to me that there are some men who cannot—how did he say?—'cannot rise above their biology.' He understands men like Antonio very well. You know, Antonio is just like a big child. John is so . . . he is established. He knows himself."

John, as it turns out, asked Isla to meet him for drinks.

"Are you going to do it?" I asked with a sinking feeling. If Gigi were to catch wind of it, she'd probably never forgive her, and our little support group would be permanently fractured. And if Isla let slip something about Gigi to John, she could ruin Gigi's life. What if John found out that Gigi had a son—possibly *his* son?

"No way," Isla said. "Don't you worry, I am not going to say anything about this to Gigi. Even if he is a nice guy, we have to keep him away from her. Just in case."

Isla closed her eyes and leaned her head back.

I stole a long look at her, searching for clues about what she was thinking and wondering how well I really knew her.

11

Delights from external objects are wombs of suffering.

—THE BHAGAVAD GITA

"Each of us has to pick a different style for her baby," Gigi announced. "My Charles is preppy. Azula is Euro. Nate is Frenchy. Honor is earthy. Anna is . . . arty!"

Arty, I thought, *a nice euphemism for hand-me-downs.*

Shopping with the yoga mamas always presented a special dilemma. Formerly a sample-sale queen, I just didn't *do* retail. But tagging along with the other mamas gave me such a contact high. On a brisk December morning we all grabbed taxis and headed to that Mecca of children's shopping known as Madison Avenue. Our first stop: Frère Jacques, the über-clothier of jet-setting babies.

With its French country theme, Frère Jacques evoked nostalgia for a perfect European babyhood at some point in an unspecified past.

I spotted an exquisite coral-hued party dress with sophisticated pleats, perfect for a penthouse cocktail party in Monaco. I pictured myself in a matching adult version, sipping a glass of pink champagne, taking in the afternoon sun, while Anna scrambled around in her frock, attracting the attention of junior royals and the children of tax-evading movie stars. I flipped open the price tag: $185.

"May I help you?" A saleswoman materialized.

"Yes," I stammered. "Is this on sale?"

"That *is* the sale price," she sniffed.

"Oh, it's for a *six*-month-old," I said, trying to sound regretful that my child was growing at such a healthy pace. Stroking Anna's head, which poked out of the top of the Björn, I handed back the precious frock. The saleswoman wasn't letting me off so easy.

"Let me check," she said. "I think we have larger sizes in the back."

"Oh, good," I said with false enthusiasm.

A few moments later, she returned. "Three years is our last," she said officiously and I tried to look sorrowful. Fortunately her attention was diverted by a man in a brown leather jacket with a handlebar moustache who was shuffling through a rack of baby dresses. She veered off in his direction, in search of more profitable prey.

"Now we're talking!" Gigi had spotted a rack of tiny seersucker suits. "This is *so* Metro!"

"Metro" for Gigi meant Metropolitan. She, too, was determined to secure a place for her boy in New York's swankest, best-dressed preschool.

Margaret held up a pair of corduroy overalls for Gigi's approval. Gigi shook her head. "It's a bit Little Red, if you know what I'm saying." The Little Red Classroom was a "progressive" downtown school founded in the early '70s by union organizers, folksingers, and *Village Voice* reporters. It was last on Gigi's list, her "safety school."

"Look at this!" Isla said, approaching with a dark blue sweater and tiny matching skirt.

"Very, uh, Metro?" I volunteered.

She wrinkled her nose. "I think it is more Holy Virgins of the Sacred Heart."

Everyone was buying things except for me. I simply couldn't afford to blow $89 on a sweater Anna could only wear for a month or two. Even the socks were $22 a pair—priced to keep people like me far away. I fingered a pair of baby mittens: $48. How could anyone spend $48 on a pair of mittens the size of cotton balls? Then I felt the smooth merino wool, perfectly contoured to fit baby's hands, and admired the delicate shade of chartreuse. Head spinning, I imagined a winter jaunt to Gstaad in the Swiss Alps, my manservant fishing things out of my trunk, while I frolicked in the snow with my little princess.

I bought the mittens.

Our next stop: Regatta, a baby emporium that specialized in outfitting your tot for a field trip to the Princeton-Yale rowing match. Nautical motifs dominated the store. One showcase featured a sailor suit hanging over the railing of daddy's yacht. Another display set rested in a giant steamer trunk—as if our babies were about to set off aboard a transatlantic cruise ship for a Grand Tour.

We oohed over a $600 christening dress, and aahed at striped cashmere sweaters for $350. We stood in awe before the pièce de résistance, a $2,000 titanium stroller. "Light enough to navigate the most challenging urban terrain," said a slightly sour saleswoman.

I wandered around listlessly, showing Anna all the clothes she would never wear. Then I made one of those finds that gives shopping a good name: At the bottom of a pile of sale items, I discovered a handmade cashmere baby sweater for $25.

"It has a hole in one of the arms," a saleswoman said with a shudder.

I searched frantically for the hole; it was infinitesimal. The sweater was *perfect*. I showed it to Anna before handing over my cash and whispered, with a sense of triumph, "Someday, you'll know what it means to win at shopping."

Margaret and Susan took my place at the sales counter. The cashier finished bagging Margaret's hoard and was moving on to Susan, when Gigi tugged my arm. "I don't like the look of that guy," she said.

Hovering next to Margaret was the moustachioed man I had seen earlier. He was standing near a rack of socks by the cash register, but he didn't seem interested in the merchandise. He didn't have the anxious look of a new father, we agreed, nor the indulgent one of a grandfather. We could see that he was glancing surreptitiously in the direction of Margaret and Susan. "I saw that guy at Frère Jacques," I said.

"He's following us?" Gigi's eyes popped open in amazement.

We slid stealthily over toward Margaret. Gigi whispered in her ear. Margaret clenched her teeth. "I bet he's a private investigator," she snarled. "That's just like Jonathan. He's already subpoenaed all my financial records, claiming I make so much money I don't need child support. Now he's probably snooping on me to get evidence for his case!"

Gigi pushed her stroller in the direction of the man. "Hey," she growled at him, "you looking for something?" He seemed taken aback. "You can tell Jonathan I'll see him in court!" Margaret barked. We had him surrounded.

"Excuse me, ladies, I don't know what you're talking about," the man mumbled. Then he spotted an opening and dashed out of the store.

"That's just the kind of tactic Jonathan uses in commercial litigation," Margaret said. "He's always hiring these thugs to follow around CEOs, catch them doing something wrong. He's practically got a whole agency on his company's payroll." We took turns patting Margaret on the back and reassuring her that buying clothes for her son was not a capital offense. "I'm not scared of that dick," Margaret said defiantly. "C'mon, let's get outta here!"

As we strolled out of the store, however, Gigi whispered a more frightening theory in my ear. "What if John sent him?" she asked.

"There's no way he saw you that day," I assured her. In fact, I thought, recalling the practiced air with which he'd flirted with

Isla, it was likely there had been so many women since Gigi, he didn't even remember her name. I reached my arm around Gigi's long, lean waist. "He didn't come for you," I said. "That was Margaret's dick, just like she said."

Gigi pushed her stroller. She was quiet, but I could see from her shifting facial expressions that the debate continued to rage in her mind.

12

When you find that you are straining, whether in a
yoga pose or in life, you are probably trying too hard.

—BARON BAPTISTE, *JOURNEY INTO POWER*

"Do I have to go?" Richard asked, like a sullen teenager.

The yoga mamas were having our first annual holiday party at
Extra Virgin, and the yoga papas had been invited. "Yes," I in-
sisted. "New fathers need support too." Besides, I told him, he
might befriend some of the other papas. Maybe he'd even meet
up with one of those papas for a weekend brunch date with the
kids and give me a chance to sleep in.

Richard sighed. "I'll come later," he mumbled and dove back
into his reading.

Annoyed, I strapped Anna to my chest and left the house.

Antonio had little trouble finding room for us; his restaurant was still struggling. Actually, it was becoming known as a place for modeling agency rejects to meet men in the throes of midlife crises. As Gigi and I walked through the terra-cotta "tasting bar," we saw only a smattering of patrons—mainly single, hungry-looking men reeking of too much cologne. Antonio greeted us in the rear of the restaurant, where he had set up a buffet-style table in the center of the room and scattered around a few chairs. Dusty agricultural implements arranged on one wall were meant to make the space look like a Tuscan farmhouse interior, but the effect was more woodworking shop. "You look fabulous! No one would guess you two were ever pregnant!" His eyes lit on me and rested a little longer than good manners allowed. There was something in his attention that felt a little naughty, like he was bending a rule to its limit, just enough to see what you would do.

Gigi showed her appreciation with a snort. "And nobody would ever guess you had your head slapped when Isla was in labor!" she said. "Looks like it's all better now." She reached over and patted him lightly on his hairless dome.

Antonio laughed and squeezed Isla, who had pulled up next to him balancing her baby in one arm and a mountain-sized plate of fusilli pasta with white-truffle-flavored olive oil in the other. "Isla is very special," he said with a wink.

She smiled and rolled her eyes good-humoredly.

He looked down at her plate and jumped back in mock horror. "Hey," he said, laying on his New Jersey accent. "You sure you want all that? Don't you wanna leave some for your love-ly friends?"

"Let me eat in peace!" she said, throwing him a furious glance.

"Oh, well." Antonio shrugged. "I hear there's a lot of work for plus-size girls."

Seeing my shocked expression, he added quickly, "I'm only saying that because she *asked* me to say something when she breaks her diet. If you ask me, she's perfect." Reaching around to her backside, he added, "Actually, I like a little junk in the trunk."

"It is you with the bubble butt," Isla retorted. "Why don't you take your daughter for a minute? You have not touched her in three months. You remember her name, yes?"

Antonio took the baby and cradled her gently. "Azula, daddy has a dream," he said, nuzzling her ear. "You and me, we're gonna get us a convertible and drive across the country, all the way to California. I'm gonna find me a beautiful, *young* woman. And we'll leave the bad mommy behind." He saw me watching him and his eyes twinkled, as though I was his conspirator.

I looked away, fussing with my food. Either Antonio was suffering from a catastrophically bad sense of humor or he was abusing Isla in front of her friends.

As Gigi and I moved away to the tasting bar abutting the room's entrance, we bumped into Susan. "Sorry I'm late," Susan said breathlessly, unwinding herself from a thick alpaca wrap and adjusting a sleeping Honor in her unbleached cotton sling. Her honey-colored hair was out of its customary ponytail and cascaded down her back. "Harcourt wishes he could come. But . . ." She shrugged her shoulders.

"What's keeping him?" Gigi asked, sounding gravely disappointed.

"He had a last-minute board meeting up at Saint Sebastian Academy."

"Harcourt spends a lot of time out of town," Gigi said.

Susan blinked. "Well, he's got so much going on. Not that I mind," she added quickly.

"But don't you need support?" Gigi asked. "Raising a baby is a big-ass job!"

"He did try to get me to hire a nanny. But I didn't want one, so I'm seeing Dr. Bruce instead."

I remembered Susan had mentioned something about seeing a therapist at one of our lunches. "Who is Dr. Bruce?" I asked.

"Dr. Bruce? He's Bruce Leyton. He's seen so many senior members of Harcourt's firm he's considered an honorary member of the board," Susan said meaningfully, as though membership on the board was on a par with winning the Nobel Peace Prize. "Dr. Bruce says I'm monopolizing Honor to compensate for a troubled relationship with my mother," she said, sounding a little bewildered.

"Really?" I asked. "What does he mean by that?"

"Well, Dr. Bruce says I'm smothering Honor. He says it's a form of anger. He says . . . he says I sometimes send out signals of hostility, even when I'm not aware of it." Susan suddenly looked uncertain.

I felt something between confused and appalled. Of all the yoga mamas, Susan was the only one who had never expressed an ounce of frustration at all the work required to care for an infant! Why would a therapist try to cast her devotion as pathology? As Susan started chatting with Isla and Antonio, Gigi and I moved back in the direction of the buffet table.

"Harcourt always has some lame excuse," Gigi said. "Can't he even make a *little* effort? And what's up with the shrink?"

I confessed that even though I had only spoken with Harcourt once, by phone, I didn't like him either. I didn't mention my conversation with Jessica at the park. I wondered if she was up at Saint Sebastian for the evening as well? Anna's weight was beginning to put a strain on my lower back, so we sat down. A few minutes later, Milton arrived. He scooped up baby Charles from his wife and sat down by my side, bouncing his son on his knee. We cooed at each other's children and offered comments that new parents use as code for: "My child is a genius, but I can see that your child isn't that far behind."

"Charles is so active!" I commented. "He's so engaged with the world."

"And look at Anna. She's so alert!" Milton replied. "Look at those eyes; she's taking it all in!"

Even though I knew he was indulging me, I flushed with pride. I turned my attention back to Charles, this time scrutinizing his face and then Milton's, searching for a family resemblance. The boy really was the spitting image of his mother.

Milton launched into a detailed discussion about the market for futures in orange juice. "The Florida crop is coming in great this year, no frost, Spain is a bust, Brazil is a question mark, and with interest rates dropping and the dollar rising, we think there are some great opportunities to arbitrage the June-July deliveries. . . ."

The world juice market turned out to be far more complicated than I'd ever imagined. As far as I could tell, Milton's firm traded futures contracts for millions of gallons of orange juice, siphoning off a gallon here and a gallon there in commissions. He was fast making his name as the Orange Juice Man on Wall Street. It wasn't the most glamorous or remunerative corner on the street, but it was enough to make a wholesome living.

Margaret's boy, Nate, swung by, in the care of his nanny, Michelle. Margaret had sent them ahead while she finished up at the office. Milton snatched up Nate and bounced him on the other knee. "Hey there, champ," he said.

Milton was the only yoga papa I'd ever seen holding two babies at once. "You look like a natural, Milton," I joked. "You want to give my husband some tips?"

Milton laughed, giving his boy a squeeze.

"Looks like you're getting ready for another one," I said.

"Working on it," he said, glancing over at Gigi at the bar. "I always wanted enough to get up a game of touch football." He saw Gigi downing a large gulp of wine and added, without much conviction, "We've got time."

Overhearing us, Gigi came over. "I gotta be honest," she said. "If we're gonna have another baby, I have to quit drinking again. And to tell the truth, that ain't gonna be easy."

"Anyway," Milton said, "how about you? Ready for a second one yet?"

"Not quite yet," I said. I always assumed I'd try for a second child. When Richard and I spoke about the future, we always referred to "kids" in the plural. But I wanted to give Anna plenty of time to enjoy all of my attention. "But we're probably going to start working on it soon."

Gigi, her wineglass held loosely in one hand, turned to me.

"You must be *crazy* to even think of having another one," she said. "I mean, you're always telling me Richard isn't doing enough as it is! That's not going to change with number two. You'll just be twice as bitter! You may as well file for a divorce right now!"

"But . . . but . . ." I sputtered. I was floored.

On the one hand, she was right. I *was* resentful and bitter much of the time . . . but Richard was gentle and brilliant and I knew that there was a lot he could teach our children. Furthermore, even though caring for Anna was sometimes bone-crushing work, I felt as though it was the most worthwhile thing I had ever done. I couldn't imagine life without her. I couldn't really believe I'd ever regret the birth of another child. How could Gigi trample over one of the most important decisions of my life? And how could she be so loud with the secrets I had entrusted her with in private conversation?

Gigi wandered back to the bar for another drink. Giving me an uncertain smile, Milton handed Nate off to Michelle and then got up to follow Gigi. Isla came over and sat next to me. "I have something to tell you," she said in an excited whisper. "John called me again!"

I looked at her, my face still showing the sting of Gigi's harsh words.

"We are only talking," she said a little defensively. "John listens to me, and he understands how I am feeling. He is so different from Antonio." She paused for a moment, and then said in a low voice, "And he sent me a very romantic note."

"Really?" I said with a combination of dread and curiosity. "What does it say?"

" 'Dear Isla, I would like to drink you. I promise not to spill a single drop.' "

So John was a cheeseball.

"You see how romantic he is?" Isla said, almost frantically. "Antonio has not said things to me like that since when he was chasing after me in Europe."

I studied her too-bright eyes. What was she really up to? If she was *really* looking for a new leading man, why did it have to be *John?* "Isla," I said sharply, "John's not just some random guy——"

"He makes me remember what it is to be a woman. What is wrong with that?" She got up abruptly and went back to the buffet table.

Richard showed up late. He looked disoriented as he wandered into the restaurant. He didn't seem to notice me in the back. Then he saw Isla.

His jaw dropped imperceptibly——imperceptibly, that is, to all but me.

For the first time in years, I felt the bite of sexual jealousy. It was as if I had woken up from a pleasing state of self-delusion about domestic fidelity, only to face a grim and sordid reality. I knew what he was thinking. He was lusting in his heart! While I was caring for his child, who at this very moment was whining! And to fall for a supermodel! And she was one of my friends to boot!

Or was she? Isla smiled at me from the pasta bar, but I averted my gaze.

I started to advance toward my faithless husband, armed and

ready for battle. I saw that Antonio had already introduced him to the pasta bar, and he'd loaded his plate with the white-truffle fusilli. I changed my mind; I decided to ignore him, let him see what life would be like without his wife.

To my immense frustration, he did not seem to notice my absence.

After stewing for a while, I marched over and handed Anna off to Richard in silence. He gave me a vacant look and resumed his conversation with Antonio while jiggling Anna on one arm. Antonio was speaking purposefully, gesturing wildly for emphasis. "Conceptual art has reached the limits of intelligibility," he was saying.

"I sense a return to infinite forms, a rediscovery of the baroque," I heard Richard reply.

"Exactly!" Antonio said. "My gallerist says we're headed for a kind of ironic classicism, something that embraces narrative while rejecting conventional closure."

As the men exchanged blasts of scaldingly hot air, I stalked off and sat down. I stuck my fork viciously into a plateful of rosemary-oil potatoes. The very sight of my husband enjoying himself in abstract discussion was loathsome to me. Then I heard the familiar cry. Anna's whines were like knives in my heart; it was physically impossible for me not to respond to them. But Richard merely flipped her from his right arm to his left and changed the subject from the baroque to rococo. His daughter was in misery, but he seemed oblivious.

I slammed down my plate and stomped over. "Give her to me," I snapped, glaring as I whisked the baby away. "Can't you even take care of her for five minutes?"

Richard looked at me. "She's fine. You don't have to flip out every time she clears her throat."

"Well, excuse me for wanting to stop my child from crying," I hissed. "I'm only following my parental instincts." Pause. "Some of us have them."

Richard turned away and started talking about the Death of Art. Seeing my distress, Susan took my arm gently, and I allowed her to draw me away. She seemed to have read my thoughts. "It's the Y chromosome," she said with a sympathetic look. "They're all that way."

It soothed me to pretend that Richard was congenitally incompetent. But in truth, I believed he was just being lazy and selfish.

Richard sauntered over, and Susan gracefully excused herself. "Hey," he said warily.

I glared at him. "You and Antonio have so much in common," I said sarcastically.

"Antonio has very interesting ideas about art," he replied. He looked around. "Not what I would have expected from a guy who runs a singles bar. He and Isla seem to have a good thing going," he added thoughtfully. "Where'd he find her, anyway?"

I was preparing to fire off a round of assault weapons at my perfidious husband when my attention was distracted. A short, stocky man wearing a pea-soup-green sweater was standing at the entrance to our private party. "Excuse me," he said brusquely. "I'm looking for Michelle Rogers."

"That's her over there," Richard said, pointing to Margaret's nanny.

The man pushed his way into the crowd of yoga mamas and papas, bumping up against Isla, who was holding Azula. The baby was unhurt but when Isla looked at him, expecting an apology, he wordlessly continued past her. "That son of a deformed she-rodent!" she exclaimed under her breath in Spanish.

The man came to a stop in front of Michelle, who was playing with Nate on a banquette. As the man loomed over her, Michelle picked up the infant and held him close.

"Michelle Rogers?"

"Yes?"

He pulled out a sheaf of papers and threw it at her feet. "You have been served." He turned and marched out. Michelle was shaking.

I handed Anna to Richard and scanned the top sheet of paper. It was from the New York City Family Court. Jonathan had decided to call Michelle as a witness in the child support case. I tried to comfort Michelle, but she kept saying glumly, "They're going to deport me." Michelle was was from Trinidad and apparently working on a forged visa. Somehow, Jonathan had found out. It was dirty pool . . . and I felt a surge of bile toward this Jonathan. How could he threaten his own child's caregiver?

Gigi got Margaret on the phone at her office and gave her the news. I could only imagine the stream of invectives pouring into Gigi's ear as she listened grimly to Margaret on the other end. "Don't sweat it, babe," Gigi reassured her. "We're gonna fight for you. We got your back here. All of us, we got your back."

13

Drop the illusion that you are covering your heart—
the secrets that you think you are hiding are exactly
what show anyway.

—RODNEY YEE, *YOGA: THE POETRY OF THE BODY*

When Isla announced that she'd hired an au pair, I knew she was
having an affair.

"Paola is *so* good with the baby, and Azula loves her," she said
with the tone of voice I'd heard other women use to express the
overt relief and unstated guilt that comes with leaving their child
in another woman's care. "I have been going to castings again.
Paola loves the guest room. I forgot what it is like. . . ." She left
the rest of the sentence unspoken, but my mind was furiously
filling in the blanks.

We were at Indochine, a lower Manhattan restaurant with

Franco-Vietnamese food, bamboo trees in every corner, and a very lively bar scene. It was our first yoga mama no-babies-allowed girls' night out, and I felt strangely untethered. Surprisingly, Richard had welcomed the chance to stay in with Anna alone. "Now don't forget to burp her after you feed her—" I had started to instruct as I pulled on an old pair of stilleto-heeled boots. "I can do it! Just go!" he said, sounding annoyed as he waved me away.

"Let him get used to it, girlfriend," Gigi said, taking a long swig of her drink.

Susan and Margaret clucked their approval, and I grinned. It felt odd to be without Anna on my chest, almost as though I was missing a limb. Yet I also felt thrillingly free. It was a giddy combination of emotions.

Isla showed up late, looking about seven feet tall in a slinky black top and beaded slides.

"Did you do a little retail therapy?" Gigi asked, admiringly.

Margaret piped up. "You should have *seen* her in action. She came to the office yesterday during lunch hour and we ran over to Barneys. She was on a mission. Two pair of shoes, that top, and this totally hot dress. And then there was the lingerie."

"Lingerie!" we chortled in unison.

"Yeah," Margaret continued with a smile, "she did some *major* damage in that department. Girls, we're not talking Jockey briefs."

"Sexy underwear." Susan giggled shyly. "That could only mean one thing."

"Lucky Antonio!" Gigi quipped. Then she added, "Poor Milton. I'm still wearing maternity panties."

"Well, none of my bras fit me after I stopped breast-feeding Azula."

Of course, I thought. *She'd have to wean her baby.*

"How is Azula taking it?" I asked. "The weaning, I mean," I added quickly.

"She is fine." Isla raised an eyebrow slightly. "Anyway, I had no choice. If I would keep on feeding," she said, "with these breasts full of milk the only photo shoots I could do would be *Playboy.*"

"Just look at her," Gigi said playfully. "She's drop-dead gorgeous, lives in a fabulous loft, and she's the nicest person you'll ever meet. If I didn't love her," she practically shouted, "I'd hate her!"

Isla gave her a good-natured grin, but I caught a flicker of panic. *Suspicion confirmed.* She stood up and looked in the direction of the ladies' room. I caught her eye and got up too.

"I'll keep you company," I said.

Isla stepped into a stall, and I stepped up to the mirror and opened my little evening bag. "So," I said, reapplying my lipstick. "How is it?"

"How is what?" Isla asked from inside the stall.

"How is your 'friend'?" I asked. She was silent. "Isla, I'm not stupid. I know what's going on."

"What do you know?" she asked sharply.

"I *know,*" I said. "Don't worry, I'd never say anything."

Isla flushed the toilet and stepped out of the stall. "I will tell you this, Laura, but you can never tell anyone else," she said in a low, excited voice.

"Of course," I reassured her, but in the back of my head an old church lady wagged her finger violently at the two of us.

"He is such an amazing lover," she said, her eyes bright. "His hands! His mouth! The way he smells! We met today for lunch, and we did not even finish eating. We went right to the hotel. He booked us at the Mercer," she added coyly.

At the mention of Soho's swankest hotel I caught my breath. News of an affair was heady, but the idea of lolling around in a luxuriously appointed suite, reclining on crisp bed linens that someone else had washed and ironed, maybe catching a little sleep—now that was enviable! "How *was* it?" I asked. *I bet they're Frette sheets,* I thought.

"Wild and with all these crazy positions! It is good I'm back to the yoga, all that stretching!" She giggled. "I'm having fun again. It is such a long time."

She looked fresh and alive. Standing in front of me I saw the confident young model who had moved to New York, convinced the world was hers. "Antonio and I, we almost don't make sex anymore," she continued. "After seven years"—she lifted her hands in exasperation—"Antonio is always too tired. And when he is awake, he does not try to please *me*."

"You've been together a long time," I said, striving for neutrality. Isla's actions felt threatening, not just to her relationship but somehow to mine. "Does John say anything about your *situation?*" I asked.

"What situation?"

"Antonio and Azula."

"He does not," she admitted. "Maybe he does not want to think about my life apart from him? He does not say much about his life apart from me. He is a little mysterious. I wish I could talk to Gigi about him." She sighed. Then she turned to me. "Laura, I think maybe I am telling you something you do not want to know."

Looking at her, my worry softened into empathy. "Isla, you seem so happy. I know it's been tough with Antonio. I'm not judging you. I just don't want . . . I just want everything to work out OK."

"I am happy to have a friend that I can talk to about this." Isla smiled at me. "You know, that red lipstick is very nice on you."

When we returned to the table, the other girls were talking about love over a scattering of appetizers. Susan was holding up a green-curry escargot on a toothpick and saying, "Sometimes, there's a moment when you just *know*. When I saw Harcourt on the beach ten years ago . . ."

"We know, sugar," Gigi said with a good-natured roll of the eyes. "But what about *before?*" She clamped down on a fried frog leg and looked around at us all. "I mean, let's forget about hubbies for a minute."

Susan gave her a blank look for a moment. "Gosh," she said, as though grasping a fading memory, "I mean, I had boyfriends in high school. . . ."

"What about you?" Gigi turned to Margaret.

Margaret chewed on her shrimp dumpling. "There was Nick, but that was before Jonatha—" She cut herself short.

"Oh, Margaret, I'm sorry," Gigi said.

"No, really, it's fine," Margaret said. She looked hurriedly down at a plate of stuffed octopus.

"Laura, your turn," Gigi said quickly.

"It would have to be Len," I said. "I'm still not sure if it was love or a train wreck."

Gigi nodded. "Been there," she said. She shook her head. "And it wasn't pretty."

"Really?" I asked. "When was that?"

"With John!" she exclaimed, as though surprised she had to state the obvious.

Margaret and Susan looked confused—Gigi was a little drunk, and seemed to have forgotten that only Isla and I knew the story of John. I stole a look at Isla, but she stared down into her wine-glass. The waiter brought us the main course, distracting us from our game. Isla never had to take her turn.

When I got home, I found Richard lying on our bed. Anna was dozing on his chest and he was gently stroking her little wisps of hair. I looked at him and was flooded with relief and gratitude for his love. I lay down next to my husband and he embraced me with one arm. "Did you have fun?" he asked.

"Yeah," I replied.

He smiled sleepily. "We missed you. Super-mommy."

And the three of us drifted off, just like that.

14

People don't allow you to sit and watch your breath.
You have to do that on your own time.

—RODNEY YEE, *YOGA: THE POETRY OF THE BODY*

When she was four months old, Anna finally accepted the reality of sleep. No longer did she fret for an hour before dozing off. Her middle-of-the-night wake-up calls dwindled until she was able to make it through to morning with only the occasional top-up from my sleepy breast.

At five months she learned to sit up, and at about the same time she learned to flip over from one side to the other. "Look at this amazing trick," Richard said, as he gleefully positioned her for a back roll across the bed. "What an athlete!"

At seven months she blew us away by crawling for the first

time. Actually, it was more like a "virtual crawl," as Richard put it, since she usually ended up back where she had started. That didn't matter; clearly our child was a genius. We were parents in love, and I felt as close to Richard as a pillow in its case.

But at times, I wanted to pick up the pillow and whack him.

The day-to-day frustrations of childrearing, and especially the household chores, were wearing me down. In my opinion, Richard was not pulling his load. I did what had to be done: the endless, mindless chores of cleaning and laundry and grocery shopping, swallowing bitter pills of discontent, while my husband lounged around reading his books and newspapers; eating meals with two hands, and making regular trips to the gym. Before the baby, our relationship had oozed stability and true partnership. Housework had *never* been an issue. I was aware that I did more, sure, but there never seemed to be that much to do, and there was plenty of time for other things. After baby, everything changed. I barely had time to bathe anymore, and our new, regressive "roles" led to arguments that lingered.

I missed earning my own money too. Before baby, my income had been slightly higher than Richard's. I'd be earning more now, I reminded myself, if Richard would pick up some of the child care and housework and allow me more time to pursue different career avenues. The injustice galled me.

More than anything, though, I missed a sense of shared interests. I missed my old best friend. Whenever I tried to address these issues, Richard accused me of being a "nag." So I turned around and nagged him some more. After a while, I realized that the more time I spent out of our house—and away from

Richard—the happier I felt. So I left the apartment as often as possible, strapping Anna to my chest for Mommy & Me yoga class—even though Anna's constant demands usually meant that I got precious little yoga out of the class—and long walks. I fantasized about bringing my husband to justice in an imaginary Court of Domestic Unhappiness. I pictured Richard cowering behind the witness stand while my lawyer—a severe and petite redhead in high-necked business attire—pointed a righteous finger at him. "Did you, on the night of November twenty-third, pretend to sleep while your daughter was crying, knowing that your sleep-deprived wife would have to get up and take care of her?" He whimpered for yes. "Did you, on the evening of November twenty-fifth, end your pathetic one-hour baby-sitting shift half an hour early just so you wouldn't have to change your daughter's heavily soaked diaper, because you *knew* that there were no diapers in the house?"

Sometimes I allowed myself to wonder if Isla hadn't found the right solution. Isla and John were apparently screwing their way through the better hotels of lower Manhattan. She called me to report on the erotic details, though at this point I was still more interested in the luxurious hotel amenities. "John took me to Soho House today," she said, giggling, on the phone late one evening. "He wanted to have sex in the steam room."

"Was it big?" I asked.

"Maybe a little bit on the big side," she replied.

"Shiny?"

"I suppose." She sounded slightly embarrassed.

"Did it smell like eucalyptus?"

"You mean the steam room?" Isla laughed. "Laura, you really need a relax!"

I didn't really want an affair; I just wanted a good night's sleep. I was hopeful that Richard and I would be able to work though this rough patch. But Isla's liaison with John marked another sort of milestone in my relationship with my husband: It was the first real secret I'd kept from him. And I was glad of it. Why does he deserve to know everything about my life anymore? I asked myself.

The yoga mamas were now gathering once or twice a week for playdates in each other's houses—every house except mine, of course, which had room for no more than two guests at a time. We would place our babies together on a mat so they could inspect stuffed dinosaurs, empty water bottles, and each other. Our tots thus occupied, we mamas could relax and talk.

In February, we all received handwritten invitations to a playdate from Jessica. Our sometimes–yoga colleague, not surprisingly, had signed up with Gaia in her new yoga studio. Jessica could barely manage the Child's Pose; she just wanted to be in the same class as Susan, as everyone but Susan could see.

The occasion for the playdate was the completion of the renovations on Jessica's TriBeCa loft, which had gone one year and several hundred thousand dollars over plan. We decided the invitation was acceptable. If nothing else, we were all curious to see what kind of loft you could get in TriBeCa for three million dollars—Jessica was never shy with numbers.

I arrived at Jessica's door carrying Anna in my BabyBjörn, as always. She was getting feisty, so to calm her down, I pulled up my shirt and popped out a breast.

"You're still carrying your baby in that?" Jessica greeted me. "And still breast-feeding?" She averted her eyes from my suckling infant. "How old is she again?"

She knew exactly how old Anna was; she was born the same week as Cameron.

"It would be different if you had a nanny," she added. "Nannies get them on a *schedule*. Helps with their independence. Got to get them ready for preschool, you know." I winced. She sounded like Richard, and ever since that faux-British phone call, I had done nothing to prepare for my daughter's educational career. Jessica grabbed my arm and took me on a well-rehearsed tour of her loft.

The place was decorated in shades of white—white walls, white furniture, white fixtures, white throw rugs, and whitish-blond wood flooring. Jessica was dressed to match, in white corduroy jeans and an off-white cashmere sweater. She had a thing for triangles, too—they were everywhere. There were gilt-framed triangular mirrors on the walls, triangular lamps, and strange white marble triangles inlaid in the wood flooring. The dining room table was a long white triangle. My new-mother's eye saw sharp points aimed like daggers at my baby.

"Our decorator is still thinking about flipping the sofas," Jessica said, gesturing at two off-white couches arranged in an L-shape in the living room.

The kitchen was fitted with restaurant-grade appliances. The stainless steel refrigerator was big enough to store a cow, and the range was big enough to cook it. But from the kitchen's spotless look, I could tell that Jessica and her husband didn't do much cooking. Even this playdate was being catered—a uniformed waiter walked around offering bite-sized canapés on a silver tray.

The apartment had several acres of space, but most of it was absorbed into the Kansas-sized living area. There was only one real bedroom; frosted glass panels marked off a second, triangular alcove that served as Cameron's room. The tot was asleep in his crib, and a glum-looking nanny sat next to him, reading *People* magazine.

"Too bad Cameron's missing the playdate," I whispered.

"I know," Jessica said. "But he had his French class this morning, and he came home exhausted."

We turned to leave, and then Jessica paused to show me the "nannycam," a small video camera in one corner of the alcove. It fed a digital signal to a laptop computer, which in turn broadcast the signal over a wireless home network.

"You can log in to any computer on the network or via the Internet, and check on baby—or nanny!" Jessica enthused, well within earshot of Cameron's caregiver. "Steve logs in from work sometimes. In fact, this icon—" She pointed at the screen. "—tells you he's logged on right now! Hi, Stevie darling!"

Suddenly a live image of Jessica's husband filled up the screen. "Hi, Jessie, I just flipped you guys on. Hope the party's going well. I'll be back late."

"Alright, darling, go back to the salt mines," Jessica chirped at the screen, as Steve signed off. "You can't leave these things to chance," she said, turning to me.

"We had to get rid of the last nanny," she whispered, still loud enough for her caregiver to hear. "I mean, I can't allow a nanny to just sit there and watch her breath. She can do that on her own time."

The bell rang, and Jessica darted to the door. Susan and Gigi had arrived. Jessica grabbed Susan by the arm and said, "Let me give you the grand tour!"

"Did I tell you my Charles is in the *Social Register*?" I heard Gigi say as they headed off.

I sat down on one of the fluffy white couches and eyed the wide-screened TV, which Jessica had tuned to a dressage competition. As I watched the well-dressed horses prance, I tried to keep Anna from staining the sofa with any of her bodily fluids.

Margaret arrived next, wearing a beige sweater and pearls. She made her way over to the couch and thrust Nathan in my face. "Smell that," she demanded. The faint aroma of aged baby vomit was unmistakable. "That's what Nate's so-called 'father' thinks is good parenting."

Jonathan was now taking care of Nate one day and one night twice a week. This did nothing to redeem him in Margaret's eyes.

"When I picked Nate up, his diaper was full of poop! He had serious diaper rash."

On top of that, she complained, Nathan was crying in his high chair, but instead of comforting him, Jonathan left him alone, "to let him cry it out." She paused for effect. "Nate cried so hard that he puked." She made bug eyes of disgust. " 'After that, he calmed down,' " she added, mimicking Jonathan.

I had my doubts about Jonathan's parenting skills too. From what Margaret told me, he had no crib, no changing table, and no toys. He refused to keep baby food in the house and insisted on trying to feed Nate whatever *he* felt like eating, which was usually Chinese takeout.

"Last week when Michelle picked him up, she told me there was some tacky girl in his apartment, all dolled up and cooing over Nate, like she was trying to prove to Jonathan how maternal she is," Margaret fumed. "I don't want *some other woman* using my baby to play house! And I don't want Jonathan pimping Nate!"

There *is* something irresistible about a man with a baby. Whenever Richard took Anna for a stroll, he'd come back to boast about how many women fawned over him. It was maddening, because my experience had been that New Yorkers view a woman with a baby as an inconvenience. I routinely got shot dirty looks.

"You know he still denies that he sicced that private detective on us," she added. "I asked him, what's the point of lying?" She gave the baby another sniff, shook her head, then asked where the bathroom was. I pointed it out and she carried Nate off to clean him up. Susan had finished the tour, and she joined me on the couch.

"How is it going with Dr. Bruce?" I asked, partly to make conversation, partly because, given the troubles Richard and I were having, the subject of therapy was suddenly interesting to me.

"I'm not sure," Susan said. A deep worry line appeared across her forehead. "He says motherhood is very demanding." Then she lowered her voice. "He says I have a condition——"

"Early-childhood burnout?" I quipped.

Susan didn't smile back at me. "I don't *want* to take antidepressants," she continued, sounding a note of defiance. "Now he wants to see me twice a week."

I suspected Dr. Bruce was just another drug-happy therapist. But then again, who was I to say? Susan did seem fairly out of touch when it came to certain things, like her marriage. Maybe her problems went deeper than I knew.

The front door opened and in stepped Isla in a flowing red poncho. Azula was on her hip in a matching tot-sized cape.

"Gorgeous outfit," said Jessica. "Tour?"

"Maybe later," Isla said breezily. "Now I must sit!" She flounced past Jessica and headed toward me with a wide, conspiratorial smile.

"What's up?" I asked.

"I had breakfast in bed at the Gansevoort," she sang into my ear.

"Continental or American?" I asked.

She gave me a pitying look.

The room had filled up with a number of moms and nannies and babies—Truman, Olivia, Zane, Bella, Jett, Luca, Ginger—I'd never met. One woman ran after her toddler from one end of the room to the other, yelling, "Hilton Theodora, come here. Hilton Theodora, stop scratching. Not in your mouth, Hilton Theodora!" There was also another Anna, which made me grimace. Since I'd capitulated to Richard's choice, it seemed as though every time I went to the park, I heard some parent or nanny saying, "Good girl, Anna," or "Come here, Anna." The city was overrun with miniature Annas. I should have insisted on Shirodhara, I grumbled to myself, as Anna's mother—the *other* Anna's mother—introduced herself. My aggravation was complete when she revealed that she worked in the marketing department of Amalgamated Motors. *My* career as a marketing consultant was doing about as well as a dummy in a test crash. After I'd pressed her for the fifteenth time on my Cheetah proposal, Robin finally sent back a short e-mail: "Great idea. But it's just too clever for us."

Now I perused newspapers and magazines at night taking a morbid interest in articles linking a women's childbearing with poverty. My favorite was the one that said for every year a woman gives up her career for her kids, she needs five to recover lost ground. I showed that one to Richard. He muttered something about "the culture of complaint" and swatted me away. As I chatted warily with the Other Anna's Mother, I slyly established that she knew my old boss, Robin.

"Oh sure, I know her," she said laconically.

I didn't dare bring up the matter of the Cheetah convertible, which would only lead the conversation to my failed *lose the baggage* suggestion. I felt a surge of utter uselessness. Somehow, this woman had managed to keep up her career, whereas I had allowed mine to wither and die. Out of the corner of my eye I saw Jessica sidle up to Susan.

"Gaia is so profound!" Jessica gushed. "I mean, that Evil Eye pose—"

"You mean the Eagle Eye pose? Yes, Gaia knows how to access the energy of universal icons."

"By the way, you were right. The headmistress at Metropolitan is wonderful," Jessica continued. "She let me peep in and observe the two-year-olds' class. They were adorable."

"You should give Harcourt a call; he knows everybody there."

"I have a better idea—Steve and I have reservations for Tuesday at Per Se and Thursday at Jean-Georges. Why don't you ask Harcourt if either of those nights fits with his schedule?"

"Of course. It would be wonderful if Honor had a friend like Cameron in her class at Metropolitan."

Metropolitan! I had expected Susan, with her free-range thinking, to send Honor to some alternative hippie home-school collective. Or at the very least to one of the city's Rudolph Steiner or Quaker schools. Instead she had chosen the preppiest, most exclusive preschool in the city at the last minute, while I could *still* hear the snooty receptionist's voice in my ear, telling me I'd left it too late.

So this was how it worked. New York's private school system is an in club, driven by money and carefully cultivated social connections. I knew this, but it was another thing entirely to see the greasy gears of high society in action.

"Canapé?" the waiter asked, thrusting out Jessica's silver tray.

As I exited Jessica's building, I noticed a man in a hat and a navy jacket across the street smoking a cigarette. He looked like the man who had been trailing us on our shopping expedition. But I couldn't be completely sure it was him. My heart pounding, I wrapped my arms around Anna, who was gurgling on my chest. "Hush," I whispered to her.

Margaret had long since left the party. Either this gumshoe wasn't after her or he was hopelessly incompetent. Or he was just another middle-aged suburban shopper, waiting distractedly while his wife ratcheted up their credit card debt a few notches. *Or* had Gigi's suspicions been proved correct? Was the PI—if that's what he was—sent by John to trail her? I turned toward the building trying to linger unobtrusively while I made up my mind what to do. *Should I warn Gigi?* I turned back to look at the man one more time. He had moved on.

When Gigi appeared, I kept quiet.

15

Inner beauty radiates from within.

—CHRISTY TURLINGTON, *LIVING YOGA: CREATING A LIFE PRACTICE*

When Anna was ten months old, I found myself chanting the old yoga slogans under my breath. I missed Gaia's class. The relentlessly cheerful Mommy & Me instructor at Hasharama helped me fit into my blue jeans, but the class no longer matched my mood.

"I'm craving a bit of *om shanti*," I confessed to Margaret by phone.

"I know what you mean!" she said to my surprise. "Let's call Susan."

* * *

Gaia was her usual, transcendental self, and it felt like old times as I rolled into Downward Dog, contorted my face into Lion's Breath, and assumed the Warrior positions in tandem with Margaret and Susan. Even our tots enjoyed the outing—they lolled on the floor, cooing in amazement at our dexterity. An old-fashioned ceiling fan overhead held Anna's rapt attention for a full fifteen minutes, giving me a much-needed chance to stretch out my sore back. I thought about getting one for the apartment.

After class, we strolled up West Broadway together, past the sidewalk art vendors. Margaret looked fresh and put together in a crisp athletic outfit. You'd never have guessed that she had been in the office since 3 A.M. that morning. Susan seemed subdued. She was losing weight, and her clavicle bones were now jutting sharply through her skin. "Yoga always makes me feel spiritually grounded," she said with little conviction.

"Well, you look skinny," Margaret said bluntly.

"Thanks," Susan said.

"No. I mean too skinny. Like you're starving."

Susan shrugged apologetically. "I don't know why. I eat like a horse."

Margaret pushed Nate in a Frog stroller, while Susan and I carried our charges in pouches. On LaGuardia Place, we passed a grocery store. "Wait here," Margaret said abruptly. "I need to pick up some milk." Susan and I lingered outside under the blue neon sign. We bounced our daughters up and down, trying to persuade them that they were having lots of fun. Margaret seemed to be taking a long time. I reached into my pocket and found a small bag of Teddy Puffs. I absentmindedly popped them in my own mouth, one by one. Then I went in to see if I could lend a hand.

Nathan was in his stroller, and Margaret was leaning against one of the refrigerators in a back aisle, a wistful expression on her face. She looked surprised to see me and hastily straightened some invisible wrinkles on her clothes. "Everything under control?" I ventured. I noticed that her cheeks were flushed pink. "This is where it all happened," she said quietly. Her face opened up, and she seemed like a different person. "This is the whipping cream section. This is where Jonathan . . ."

I had never heard her mention her former partner's name in such a tender way. She smiled a wide, guilty smile and I caught a glimpse of the carefree woman that had pursued her pleasure so recklessly that evening long ago.

"That was some night. Huh, Nate?" she said softly to her boy. She bent down and nuzzled him. Nate smiled in response. She gave him a tender kiss on his creamy cheek, then straightened up and turned to face me. She let out a short, sharp laugh. The moment had passed. We left the store without buying anything.

Back outside, Margaret said a hurried good-bye. "Nate's got to go down for a nap," she explained sternly. "And I *really* need to finish up those briefs."

"You have to try this green tea," Susan called from the kitchen as I played with the girls. She had invited me over, and I had gladly accepted. Anything to put off seeing Richard lying on the couch with his books.

"It's from this macrobiotic plantation in Japan. It's full of antioxidants."

She returned with two steaming mugs, and we rested them on the glass pane of a coffee table, waiting for them to cool. Susan fingered the seashells on her special necklace and Anna started opening and shutting her little palm, her newest way of communicating a request for milk. I was a bit tired of being the family restaurant. Shouldn't a ten-month-old be learning to eat in a big-girl way by now? I pulled out a bottle I had prepared earlier and offered it to her.

"Does Anna want bottle milk?" I asked hopefully. "Yum, yum!"

Anna protested furiously until I pulled up my shirt and gave her what she really wanted. Susan was already breast-feeding Honor.

"Is that cow's milk?" she asked me, with studied neutrality.

"Yes," I replied.

Susan was quiet, then said, "I've read goat's milk is easier for babies to digest."

Now it was my turn to be quiet. I would have been willing to give Anna *chocolate* milk if only she would drink it neatly from a bottle, like other babies. My overworked breasts wanted a break.

"Anyway," she continued, "if you're tired of breast-feeding you can cut down, but you shouldn't just break off. That kind of rupture in the parent-child bond can be psychically damaging, and probably leads to allergies in later life."

I nodded absently; "allergies" were a fundamental part of Susan's universe.

"Bushmen of the Kalahari Desert breast-feed until their children are four years old," she continued.

I pictured myself living in a mud hut, walking around naked from the waist up, with a pair of four-year-olds hanging from my pendulous mammaries.

"Dr. Bruce says I should stop," Susan said suddenly. "He wants me to go on antidepressants. I keep telling him that I can't because I *want* to breast-feed."

I could see that the thought of her therapist agitated her. "Is he still saying you have some 'condition'?" I asked her. She nodded. "Then why do you keep seeing him? I mean, is he helping you?" One of Anna's half-dozen baby teeth grazed my nipple and I grimaced.

"Well, Harcourt really wants me to keep it up," she said. "He promised that if I stick to it . . ." Her voice trailed off.

"If you stick to it, what?" I asked. But Susan put her finger to her lips as she rocked a dozing Honor to sleep. Susan left Honor resting on the couch and excused herself. "Just have to check on some stuff," she said. She walked into one of her bedrooms, leaving the door cracked open.

My cell phone vibrated, letting me know I had a message. Gently placing Anna—who was also nodding off—down on the couch, I walked around Susan's living room while I dialed into my voice mail. *Hello, hello, hello,* I heard Jessica's voice. She sounded jubilant. *I just had to tell everybody. Steve, my precious, darling Steve, just gave me the most fabulous anniversary present! We're here at Le Refuge, and the weather is just fantastic, and last night we were having dinner on the terrace, and when dessert came he had them bring me a Tiffany box with the most gorgeous diamond earrings I have ever seen. They are one-point-four-five carats each, D-grade, radiant cut,*

I can't wait for you to see them! I snapped my phone shut. Jessica was unbelievable.

From where I was now standing, I could see Susan in her bedroom. The room was almost monastic in its simplicity—a large double bed, neatly made, a simple wooden dresser, and two bedside tables, empty except for an answering machine and a tortoiseshell hair clip. I thought of my own bedroom, about half the size and cluttered with the detritus of married life: photographs, take-out menus, half-empty water bottles, well-thumbed *New Yorkers* that we sometimes fought over late at night. Susan was bent over her bedside table, pressing buttons on the answering machine.

Mr. Fielding has asked me to inform you that his meetings in Paris are going to be running over schedule. It was the officious voice of Harcourt's assistant. *He expects to be back in the middle of May. If you have any messages for Mr. Fielding, you can reach me at my direct line at the office, and I will relay your messages to him personally.*

The machine beeped. "Next message, received today, at nine-forty-four," said the computerized voice.

Hello, hello, hello! It was Jessica. *I just had to tell everybody. Steve, my precious, darling Steve, just gave me the most fabulous anniversary present. We're here at Le Refuge. . . .*

My stomach twisted. Susan's tenth anniversary was due in April, and *she* was the one who was supposed to spend it with her husband at Le Refuge. And now he would be in Paris instead. Jessica could not have had worse timing.

I saw Susan sit on her bed. She seemed to be staring at her knees. She started fingering her seashells. Then she put her head in her hands and rocked gently back and forth. Instinctively, I backed away from the bedroom door and out of her view. I sat on the couch with the sleeping babies and wondered what to do. Long minutes passed. Finally, Susan emerged with slightly reddened eyes.

"Susan, I . . ."

"My allergies are really acting up," she said, smiling far too brightly.

"If there's something I can do," I said.

"Oh, no," she said, shaking her head politely. "I've been forgetting to take my vitamin pills. I'm such a goof."

I desperately wanted to break through, but Susan deflected my every effort to bring the conversation around to what was really bothering her. Finally, she stopped talking altogether, and just smiled vacantly at me. Then she yawned and said she felt like joining Honor for a nap. I nodded, gathered up my own sleeping tot, and headed for home.

16

Most men have the image of themselves that they're really quite stiff. But really where they're stiff is in the head.

—RODNEY YEE, *YOGA: THE POETRY OF THE BODY*

I'd been up since 5 A.M.

I'd changed Anna twice and fed her three times, done two loads of laundry, and washed the dirty dishes left in the sink from the night before. I made oatmeal on our kitchenette stove, stirring the viscous, bubbly stuff with one hand and holding Anna in the other. While tending the pot, I rescheduled a doctor's appointment over the phone and gathered the essentials into Anna's bag—diapers, wipes, water, snacks, and a change of clothes.

Richard rolled out of bed at 8 A.M. and ambled over to the couch, stopping to pick up the *New York Times* at our door. I brought a bowl of oatmeal over to him. His nose was already buried in the op-ed page. I tried to lower Anna into her high chair. She howled like a monkey, so I sat down at the kitchen table and put her on my lap. She immediately flailed her tiny hand against the oatmeal bowl, scattering blobs of it across the table, on the floor, and onto her pajamas. I let her nurse while I ate what remained of the oatmeal. As I cleaned the table and washed the dishes, I snarled silently at Richard. *There he was,* I thought, *keeping up on current events, while I busted my ass and my brain turned to oatmeal.* Before Anna, I used to stay abreast of world events. I even used to read books. Now, I figured, by the time Anna was old enough to have a conversation, I'd have nothing left to say. She'd chat about current events with her well-informed father, while I'd be a dried husk, fit to be thrown out with yesterday's paper.

After breakfast, I unsnapped Anna's oaty onesie and pulled it off. As I tried to wrangle a fresh onesie over her head, she screamed like a torture victim. Ever since she had learned the art of resistance at eight months, dressing her had become a painful chore. I managed to fit her head through the collar, but when I tried to guide her hands into the sleeves, she shrieked and twisted. With her arms and legs flailing in all directions, I needed some help.

"Richard, can you give me a hand?" I said sharply.

He looked up. "Do you think both of us dressing her is an efficient use of time?"

"*Efficient!*" I shouted. "Do you think it's *efficient* for *me* to do *everything* while you lie there like a *slug?*"

"Whatever." Richard threw the paper down and came over. "Let me do it," he sighed.

"We can do it together," I said, trying to avoid a fresh outburst of screams.

"Just let me!" he ordered, and held up a hand.

I headed toward the bathroom, fully aware that he would fail. Sure enough, Anna started to cry. "Maaaaaa!!" she sobbed, her face turning purple. *"Maaaa!!"* The cries hit me in the back like guilt-tipped arrows, but I resolved to make it to the bathroom anyway. After a few moments, her wailing subsided. I was grateful for the first break in my three-hour morning. *Maybe I can take a shower and wash my hair,* I thought. I grabbed one of the Le Refuge bottles from my secret stash behind the sink. There was a semi-clean towel on the back of the open door. I turned the water to scalding, just as I liked it. *Perfect.* I stepped into the steamy spray. I turned my face up toward the nozzle and let the water stream over my body. *Nirvana.* Just as I reached for the shower gel, I heard a fresh round of bloodcurdling screams. This time it sounded as though Anna was having a limb amputated. Trailing water and tangerine suds, I jumped out of the shower and poked my head around the door. I noticed the towel was gone.

"What's going on out there?" I demanded.

Richard had pinned Anna on the floor with one arm while changing her with the other. She was lying on the towel. Anna had recently decided that she didn't like being changed lying down; I dealt with this new development by frequently changing her in a standing position. It required an effort to balance her, but it was well worth it to avoid her fits. Richard, however, handled the matter by using brute force.

"Resistance is futile," I heard him say through gritted teeth. To me and, I thought, to Anna, his methods were barbaric.

"She hates that!" I yelled. "Change her standing up! That's what she wants!"

"How the hell do you know what she wants?"

"I *know* what she wants because I take care of her *all fucking day!*" I shivered with a cold rage, thinking, *asshole!* as the water dripping from my naked body accumulated in a small puddle on the floor. "You change your baby so infrequently you can't even *do it right!*"

Richard threw his hands up in the air. "OK, you take her, Psycho-mommy!"

Anna wriggled out of the diaper and crawled like a bug to the other side of the room, naked except for the onesie dangling around her neck. Freed from the constraint of her diaper, she chose that moment to drop a tankful of runny poop on the carpet. Sometimes it was amazing how much stuff she had inside of her.

I ran over and picked her up. The excrement on her legs felt warm and sticky against my cold, wet, naked body. I snatched a handful of baby wipes and cleaned both her and myself off as best I could. I held her standing up and put her diaper on. I wrestled on her onesie, pants, socks, and shoes, meeting fierce resistance all the way. Then I shoehorned her screaming into her stroller, a "pre-owned" Frog I'd put on our credit card, partly to stop the yoga mamas from carping, partly because my back was starting to give out after ten months with the BabyBjörn. But Anna didn't give a damn about my back. She hated the stroller and so she screamed some more while I quickly put my clothes on. With my body still wet, everything seemed to cling awkwardly. In that instant, I pictured my daughter as a parasite, a leechy, sucky thing that wanted only to drain the life out of me, like a tapeworm living on the outside that took semi-human form the better to fool its victim. I gave myself a mental slap in the face—how could I think such a thing? Was I a *bad mother?* Anna's cries of outrage seemed to say, *Yes, Mom, you are rotten to the core.*

I bent down as if by reflex to comfort her. "Anna," I cooed, then froze. Here I was, drowning in my sticky, slightly smelly clothes, tending to my daughter's increasingly insistent demands—and she had a name *Richard* had foisted on me in a moment of weakness. Richard, who seemed to believe that his job as a father *ended* with the naming of our child. *What made him think he could excuse himself from the work of childrearing? Had he been counting on my sense of maternal obligation all along?*

The lumpy pool of yellowish baby poop festered untouched on our carpet. I looked over to Richard and witnessed the greatest outrage of all: He was lying on the couch reading an Ancient Greek grammar book. While I was struggling to care for a child who bore *his* first name *and* his last name, he was lying on his back learning a dead language? It was more than I could bear.

"You're not going to get away with this!" I screamed.

"Get away with what?"

"You! You lazy souvlaki-sucking pig!" I said, channeling Isla.

"Hey, calm down, you're scaring Anna!"

" *'Psycho-mommy?'* If I'm crazy, Richard, it's because you drove me crazy!"

"I never said—"

"We have a two-class system in our marriage! I'm tired of being the proletariat!"

"Marxism is dead," was his response.

I threw the vacuum cleaner at him.

He got up quietly, brushed the dust off, and left for the library. "We'll talk when you're rational again," he said on his way out.

That did it. *It's over,* I told myself.

Seething, I rummaged in the closet for a small suitcase. I stuffed it with the overflow from Anna's closet: several changes of clothes, her favorite book, a plastic dinosaur. More diapers. There was a little space left in the suitcase for me. *What should I bring?* I packed some underwear and a fresh T-shirt. It didn't matter what I wore, I told myself, tearfully. What mattered was that Anna was taken care of. I'd just wear the same clothes day after day. Now that I was all alone.

I hooked the suitcase to the handle of Anna's stroller and pushed us out of the apartment. It was a beautiful summer day. I didn't know where to go. *Should I return to Mom? Should I go to the Greyhound station and buy a ticket to some nowhere town in Alabama?* I pictured myself renting a trailer with Anna, finding a job as a truck-stop waitress, putting Anna in day care, downing grim dinners of SpaghettiOs by the light of a single, naked bulb, watching Anna suffer the early stages of infant malnutrition, discovering the day-care workers were running a child porn ring. I started to cry.

I wandered aimlessly, following the stroller wherever it led me. The stroller—as if by force of habit—took me to Washington

Square Park, near the children's play area. I saw a woman walking three shar-pei dogs, a grizzled man in a purple T-shirt philosophically strumming his guitar, a young couple sharing a joint. I sat on a bench with my bag and my baby, wondering what to do. Anna cooed at the dogs and gave me an expectant look. "Things are going to be different now," I told her. "I had no choice."

She drooled and looked away. I was well and truly alone.

I pulled out my cell phone and called Gigi.

An hour later, all the yoga mamas arrived at my bench, in a caravan of Frogs. Isla unpacked some fresh-baked croissants from her local French bakery. Susan brought a large bottle of fresh-squeezed orange juice. Margaret came in her business suit, carrying a supply of plastic cups from the office but no baby. Nate was with his father, she explained. Gigi opened up her long summer jacket to reveal two bottles of champagne packed into the interior pockets.

"Let's do this discreetly, girls," she said as she poured the bubbly liquid into waiting cups. "You don't want to get me arrested!" Her eyes were too bright. I realized she had already been drinking. "Milton's such a bore," she said. "He doesn't want me to have any fun."

Susan was gaunt and listless. When Gigi placed a mimosa in front of her, she shuffled it back across the picnic table. Gigi picked it back up and slammed it down in front of Susan, allowing a few drops to splatter.

Susan held Gigi in her steady gaze. "You won't solve your problems with champagne," she said with quiet, unexpected ferocity.

Gigi's overly mascara'd eyes popped open like giant bull's-eyes. "Whoa! So you think it's better to see Dr. *Bruce?* Is he still telling you to go to a 'retreat'? Earth to Susan: 'retreat' means *nut house!*"

Susan closed her eyes and retreated into something that looked like the Mountain Prayer pose. "Hey!" Margaret said sharply to Gigi. "Let Susan work things out with her husband in her own way." She looked around the table. "What a bunch of whiners! So privileged and you don't even know it. You got everything you wanted. Husbands——"

"Don't be a fool," Isla snorted. "You can say you want a man. But all men are the same. Full of empty promises." Weary disenchantment filled her luminous eyes. The affair with John, I sensed, had failed to solve the problem of Antonio.

We stared at each other in silence, stunned by the the sudden outbreak of hostilities. The strain of ten months of motherhood, I realized, was showing on us all. The yoga mamas seemed to be dangling at the end of a rope.

Gigi slammed her drink on the table. "C'mon, guys! Look at us! We're acting like a bunch of *negative Bettys!*"

"You're right, Gigi," Susan said quietly. "We need to take care of Laura now."

"Yeah, she's our little runaway," Margaret said.

The mamas looked at me. I wanted to hug them all.

"Do you remember how we first met . . . ?" I asked.

We started reminiscing about our prenatal days. So much had changed since that first yoga class in the Hasharama studio. Those last months of pregnancy now seemed like a golden age. How wonderful it was to be big with the future, instead of burdened with the present! How special we felt when everyone—even our husbands—showed us so much respect and admiration! How easy it was to care for our babies when they were on the inside! How peaceful life seemed when we floated our pregnant bodies in a warm swimming pool at . . . *"Le Refuge!"* Gigi shouted.

The yoga mamas were electrified.

"We need it!"

"We deserve it!"

"Let's do it!"

This time, I didn't give a second thought to money. I had charge cards! I was going to run away—in style! In my mind, I was already lounging by the swimming pool, swanning around the elegant grounds, and taking in the stress-blasting "rituals." Susan especially seemed energized at the thought of returning to her old honeymoon location. Then a small cloud passed over her clear blue eyes. "Oh, I'd have to cancel my appointments with Dr. Bruce," she said uncertainly.

"Cancel them!" Gigi and I yelled in unison.

Susan smiled sheepishly. "I can always do a makeup session."

Then a much darker cloud crossed her face. "Le Refuge won't let our babies in. I can't leave Honor here with a sitter. It's still hard for me to be apart from her even for an afternoon, never mind a couple of days," she said. "I can't."

I had forgotten Le Refuge had a strict, no-children policy. I couldn't bear the thought of being away from Anna for a few days either. Anyway, I couldn't leave Anna behind if I was running away with her. Margaret, too, could not leave her child behind over the weekend. "I'm in the office all week, and Jonathan takes him on Fridays; the weekends are all the time I have."

Gigi and Isla, on the other hand, thought it would be grand to leave their babies behind for a weekend. But they wouldn't go without the rest of us. Then Susan looked at the somber mamas and said, "I've got it."

We all looked at her hopefully.

"We can sneak the babies in! The staff will never know!" I looked at her in quiet amazement. There was a note of defiance in her voice I'd never heard before.

"Screw those spa fascists!" Gigi roared. "We're bringing the babies!"

The yoga mamas were unanimous. We were going back to Le Refuge, and we were going to bring Honor, Anna, and Nate—in a clandestine operation! In the back of my mind, I knew it was all a little reckless. But I didn't care.

For the rest of that afternoon, we plotted.

Susan called her husband's office and spoke to his assistant. The assistant seemed to know about her therapy appointments and put up some resistance when asked to cancel them. But Susan insisted, and promised to make up her missed session the following week, so the secretary reluctantly agreed to make the arrangements for our stay. We agreed to meet up in a few hours, which gave the other mamas enough time to organize themselves and their babies for the trip. As I had nothing clean in my suitcase, each of the mamas promised to bring an extra tank top, bathing suit, or pair of shorts for me. A flurry of excited phone calls filled the airwaves as the mamas spread the news to husbands, nannies, and envious friends.

I didn't want to go home and risk seeing Richard. In the excitement of the moment, my anger toward him no longer seemed to press so hard upon my heart, and I knew I had to tell him I was leaving town. I wasn't really *running* away. I was just *getting* away. But I wasn't ready to talk face-to-face just yet. I wanted Richard to suffer my absence a bit; perhaps he would see the error of his ways. So I left a brief message on our answering machine instead. "Anna is fine. We will be seeking refuge for a few days. Don't call me. I'll call you."

Margaret dashed back to the office to get her affairs straightened out. The rest of us headed off in the other direction. As my bag was already packed, I planned to while away the time in the baby park while the others firmed up their arrangements.

The children's play area teemed with life, and I approached the battery of swings in the company of my friends as they headed for the gate. One swing was occupied with a boy in a tot-sized baseball hat. We could see his father's animated, adoring face as the man pushed the child back and forth.

"Here ya go!" the man was shouting happily as the boy squealed with delight. "Swing low! Swing high!" Both were obviously enjoying themselves very much.

As we approached, the man gave us a smile. We all smiled back. Few sights are more endearing to a new mother than that of a father caring for his child.

As I watched the man playing with his son, I started to audition him as the romantic lead in my own escape fantasy. *He's definitely single,* I decided, *a young widower. Nice-looking too. Perhaps he and I will build our own home together on the coast of Long Island out of beautifully varnished driftwood. . . .*

"How old?" the man said, looking at Anna.

"Ten months," I said. "And your little guy?"

"Same!"

He smiled like we'd both won at bingo, and I smiled right back. We came around to where the man was standing and I got my first good look at the boy's face. I jumped with amazement. *Nate! It was Margaret's son!* I rapidly dismantled my imaginary driftwood palace and cast it back into the Atlantic.

Gigi, Isla, and Susan recognized him at the same instant. "Nate?" they squeaked.

"So *you're* Jonathan?" said Gigi.

"Oh, ah, are you friends of the mother?"

"The mother?!" said Isla, incredulous. "The mother has a name. She is Margaret!"

"I'm well aware of that. I didn't mean to—" Jonathan started to explain defensively.

Gigi interrupted him. "Have you changed Nate's diaper yet today?"

"I think we must see if Nate is smelling," Isla snapped.

Then to my surprise, Susan cut in. "Gigi! Isla! Let's give him a chance." She turned to Jonathan. "Jonathan, it's so nice to meet you. I hope we can see you again someday." She fished out one of her calling cards and handed it to him. Jonathan absently handed Susan one of his cards while regarding Isla and Gigi warily. For a moment, there was silence. Then Isla narrowed her eyes. "We must see his diaper."

Flustered, Jonathan lifted Nate out of the swing and put him in his stroller. Nate chirped happily, blissfully unaware of the parental politics at hand. "Really got to get back home now," Jonathan muttered. "So nice to meet you," he said, looking at Susan and avoiding the rest of us. A bag filled with bottles and toys slipped from his hands and spilled its contents on the ground. He hurriedly gathered the items and stuffed them back in the bag. I caught a look of dismay on his face as he pushed his boy out of the park.

"Bye-bye, Nate," we said.

Gigi looked at Susan. "How could you be *nice* to that cretin?" she demanded.

"I think you have to understand where someone is coming from before you can judge them."

Gigi lifted her hands in exasperation. "Susan, will you get a grip?" she said. "Guys like that are creeps. Period. You don't give them a second chance. Get your head out of the sand!" Then she and Isla marched home to retrieve their things. Susan looked at me helplessly.

"Gigi shouldn't have criticized you," I volunteered.

"It's OK," said Susan. Then she seemed to relax. "She just has free-floating anger inside. It's what gives Gigi her core. It's probably left over from her difficult childhood. And it's probably what gave her the strength to overcome her family circumstances and make a better life for herself."

I stared at her, surprised. She'd made the comment entirely

without malice, as though she were observing the weather. She was nodding her head at me, and for once, I nodded back with conviction.

"Anyway," Susan said, "seeing Jonathan with Nate—I think he really loves him."

I had to agree. Margaret had led us to imagine that Jonathan was a hideous combination of Joseph Stalin and Don Juan. Instead, he looked more like a character on a sitcom—a thirty-something, average-height, easygoing, slightly goofy father with bad hair who was very much in love with his son.

"I think he means well," Susan said with finality.

17

If you have an interest in liberation, you probably
practiced yoga in previous lifetimes.

—SHARON GANNON AND DAVID LIFE, *JIVAMUKTI YOGA*

Gigi was driving the SUV ahead of us, with Susan and Honor in
the backseat. She was overjoyed to have left Charles behind with
Milton, an active daddy and the envy of the yoga mamas. How-
ever, just because she wasn't planning to smuggle her baby in did
not mean Gigi planned to be a model client at Le Refuge. "I've
got a case of wine in the trunk," she announced as we prepared to
launch our little convoy. "That no-booze rule is *insane*."

Margaret and I and our two tots were riding with Isla in Anto-
nio's black Hummer. Like Gigi, Isla had no intentions of being a
model client at Le Refuge. In her overnight bag she carried a stash

of Belgian chocolates and *jamon serrano,* cured Spanish ham. "I cannot survive on hamburgers made out of *garbanzos,*" she said. "Anyway, who do they think they are, to tell us we cannot bring our own food?" Isla had left her baby behind, although she was extremely nervous about it: Her au pair, Paola, was on holiday for the weekend. Antonio would have to take care of Azula by himself. "Maybe it is good for him to finally spend some time with his daughter. I want him to understand how much work it is, taking care of the baby. Now he will not be able to pretend to the girls at his club that he is a twenty-six-year-old in leather pants. He is a father!" But Isla wasn't letting go easily. She had a cell phone headset on, and barked instructions to Antonio all the way down the Long Island Expressway.

"Do not give her the whole blueberries, they are too big for her to eat. Cut them in half first. . . . She wants to be picked up now, I can hear her crying. . . . Did you check her diaper? . . . Why is she coughing? Open the windows! Call the doctor! . . . OK, well, don't do that to her again."

Her driving was making me a little nervous.

While Isla argued with Antonio and dodged cars on the expressway, Margaret barked into her own cell phone from the front seat. Her day in court was coming up in a couple of weeks, and she needed to get her legal team "up to speed." Margaret had instructed her nanny Michelle to pick Nate up from Jonathan's house. "That way I don't have to see his ugly face," she had said. "Plus, he has to deal with the woman he's trying to get kicked out of the country."

Next to me in the back, Anna and Nate fidgeted and fussed in their car seats. I wasn't sure which bothered them more—the cell-phone chatter or the swerving in and out of traffic. One thing for sure was that they objected to the very idea of a car seat. They were both city kids, accustomed to ten-minute rides in yellow cabs. Unlike their suburban brethren, they knew almost nothing of child-safety laws, which they would clearly have viewed as a gross infringement of their liberty. I struggled to distract them with finger puppets and egg shakers, but with limited success.

After a couple of hours on the highway, we turned off onto country roads, and the pressures of the city finally started to fade. Anna and Nate thankfully nodded off to sleep, Margaret decided her legal team was "on the same page," and Isla grudgingly accepted that Azula was not dying in the hands of her father. I watched the verdant scenery through the Hummer's wide windows and wondered what Richard was doing.

As we wound our way through the long and beautifully landscaped driveway leading up to Le Refuge, we conferred by phone with Susan in the car ahead in order to finalize the details of our planned baby-smuggling operation.

We knew the front desk faced a large, open window, with a clear view of the stretch of land we would have to cross with our unauthorized tots. We parked the vehicles in the small, tree-lined lot, some distance from the main entrance. Isla, Gigi, and I headed into the lobby, where Spa Lady greeted us in her white robe, a large crystal hanging on a silk cord around her neck. "We—that is, *Susan*—is really stressed out," I explained with an apologetic smile. The Spa Lady's eyes lit up at the mention of the all-powerful Mrs. Harcourt Fielding. "We need to unload right away," I said. "Susan can't speak to anybody now. I'll come back afterward and handle the paperwork."

The Spa Lady nodded with the sagaciousness of a thousand gurus and handed me the key. I gave it to Isla and we headed back to the cars. Gigi, as planned, stayed in the lobby, to distract the Spa Lady with questions about the spa menu. "So, tell me about this four-hand job," I heard her saying.

Isla went over to the chalet to prop the door open and flush out any enemy agents who might be placing last-minute toiletries. I scurried back to the car, and Margaret, Susan, and I loaded our still sleeping babies into straw grocery bags—the circular kind with handles on two sides. Susan had discovered that these bags, carefully padded with baby blankets, could comfortably carry a ten-month-old infant. The only way to see the baby inside was to peer straight down from overhead. I glanced over to the chalet. Isla was standing in the doorway in the Warrior One yoga position.

That was the signal. The coast was clear.

Now the trick was to slide by that big window without our babies screaming, sticking a hand out, or otherwise giving away the game. Things were looking good as we strode confidently toward the Honeymoon Chalet. Then, about halfway across the lawn, Anna started fidgeting in her sleep and let out one of her trademark wails. The Spa Lady shot us a look through the open window. Showing incredible presence of mind, Susan grabbed my shoulder and started to sob. She looked like an escapee from an insane asylum. I pretended to comfort her.

"The *poor thing!*" I heard Gigi say in the distance.

It worked. The Spa Lady shook her head sympathetically, apparently convinced that we were just one more group of distressed urbanites fleeing the pressures of the big city. I waved back in acknowledgment of her concern. At that point, Honor started whining too. Fortunately, Gigi accidentally-on-purpose knocked over a small shelf of Le Refuge body lotions, and she and the Spa Lady bent down to pick up the mess. That gave us the cover that we needed. We broke out into a trot and then slammed the door of the Honeymoon Chalet behind us, giggling with relief.

We spent the evening laughing in the chalet, downing three-bean burgers topped with *jamon serrano* and popping chocolates into our mouths. Gigi opened two bottles of wine and polished them off pretty much by herself. The kids had developed their own fraternity, playing and giggling, imitating each other's expressions and "sharing" toys. Anna mashed bananas on the bed until they turned into gooey lint-balls. I fished a few out of her mouth before she quieted down for the night.

The next morning, Susan insisted that I undergo one of the spa services. I protested, but she was firm. "You're our runaway," she said. "You need to find your inner truth."

So, while Isla and Margaret entertained the babies with our secret stash of board books and stuffed kittens, Gigi, Susan, and I padded gleefully out of the chalet. On the verdant path to the Spa Palazzo, Susan began chatting to a friendly fellow guest, an older woman with long, white hair and a robe to match. As they both tried to outdo each other in praise for Le Refuge, I caught the lady staring at the pacifier dangling from Susan's neck. "That's unusual," she said, suspiciously.

In a flash, Susan popped the pacifier in her mouth. "It's part of my regression therapy," she said effortlessly. "My life coach says it's the best way to get in touch with my inner child." Our fellow guest nodded and then headed off in the direction of the serenity labyrinth.

In the Spa Palazzo, Gigi opted for the Sensory Deprivation Tank. "I'm in the bag," she announced. "I need to turn the volume way, way down." I chose to embark on the Shirodhara-Ayurvedic Fusion Journey again. I desperately wanted to reenter the zone, to rediscover the kind of peace I had experienced at this very place when I was seven months pregnant. As my healer poured oil on my forehead and into my 'third eye', I finally started to relax. Then I caught myself humming "The Rubber Ducky Song"— one of the dozen-odd nursery tunes that had colonized my brain. I cracked open one of my eyes. The therapist was giving me a strange look. I stopped humming.

Later that morning, we traded places with Isla and Margaret. They went off on their journeys while Susan and I watched the kids and Gigi napped. Two hours and forty-nine readings of *Where Are Maisy's Friends?* later, the other mamas returned, and the Honeymoon Chalet buzzed with activity. Gigi fished another bottle of merlot out of her suitcase and Isla, who looked more luminous than ever after her Banana Wrap-ture, brought out her stash of contraband delicacies. Life at last seemed to be approaching the joyful equilibrium of our earlier days, when, suddenly, the Spa Lady burst into our chalet. Gigi was swigging red wine straight from the bottle, Isla and Margaret were pecking at the chocolate truffles and other snacks on the coffee table, and Susan and I were lying on the floor playing "flying baby" with our tots—holding them up over ourselves and swooshing them around like tiny airplanes.

We were busted.

"I knew it!" the Spa Lady gasped. "Food! Alcohol! *Babies!!*"

Anna took advantage of the distraction to twist out of my grasp. In order to catch her, I jerked my body to the right, bumping into Gigi and sending her red wine splashing all over the pristine white sofa. The Spa Lady contemplated the large purple stain as it sank into the pale wool. Horror gave way to anger.

"This is an outrage! Completely unacceptable!" she seethed. "You ladies have *lied* to me and *abused* your privileges. I am *extremely* disappointed." She glared at us. "I want you *off the premises! Immediately!*"

Then she looked directly at me and said bitterly, "Your husband would like to speak to you. Thank goodness he called. He said you might be here. He told me that you had a *baby* with you! At least *he* was sensible."

Shaking her head, she turned and stalked out.

I was livid.

"That bastard!" I cried. "He *told* on us? How could he?! I don't want to see him ever again! I'm going to move away with my baby and start a whole new life. I'll send him photos every year or two so he can see how beautiful his baby is, the one he'll never know," I ranted. "And I'll change her name. Her name is *not* Anna! It's Shirodhara!"

"Shiddy-*what?!*" Gigi gave me a look.

"Laura," Susan said sympathetically, "maybe you need to drink some tea."

"Never mind the tea," Margaret interjected. "We've got three babies, two days, one runaway, and no place to stay. What are we going to do?"

We sat quietly in the disarray of the Honeymoon Chalet for a moment. Then Susan raised her hand. "We'll go to Harcourt's family home," she said defiantly. "It's only fifteen minutes from here, and Harcourt can't complain. He's away on business, and this is an emergency."

"Are you sure?" Gigi said with undisguised hope.

The other mamas and I exchanged glances. Susan had always been discreet, but from snippets here and there we had all come to the conclusion that the Fielding Manor was a grand place indeed.

"I'm sure," Susan said firmly.

We all nodded our agreement and began packing our bags.

18

The best way of sustaining his body is for the yogi to beg his food from the highest kind of householders, i.e. the yogi must only go to the home of those who are believers, humble, of controlled mind, learned in the scriptures, and saintly.

—ALAIN DANIÉLOU, *YOGA: MASTERING THE SECRETS OF MATTER AND THE UNIVERSE*

Susan's beachfront estate was photo-shoot ready. As we rolled up the winding driveway to the old colonial mansion shaded by ancient oaks and evergreens, I was struck by the splendor in which she lived. "Schwing!" Gigi exclaimed as the magnificent, 1920s façade came into view through the manicured gardens. "That's some pile," Margaret grunted appreciatively.

A walk through the airy rooms of the main house made me forget all about Le Refuge. A lovely arrangement of hydrangeas and casablanca lilies greeted us in the sunny foyer. Classic beach-house furniture combined with lavender-scented linens added to the sense of overwhelming comfort. The house had something over ten bedrooms. "Depending on how you count it," Susan said vaguely. She ignored the charming architectural details and focused instead on the baby-friendly features. Susan had made use of professional baby proofers. A squadron of pink-suited men came over one day, she told us, and covered up the electrical outlets, padded all the sharp corners on the furniture, removed potentially lethal objects, and otherwise made the house safe for toddling tots.

As we moved upstairs to view the various bedroom suites, Susan drew our attention to the mattresses. "They're made in a biodynamic farm in Sweden from wild goose feathers," Susan explained. "But they only use feathers that fall off, so they're gathered without inflicting pain on the geese. I think it makes for sweeter dreams, don't you?" Then, with a figurative lightbulb flashing over her head, she said, "Come into my bedroom and let me show you something!" We followed behind her to the master bedroom. Ignoring the picture window with the glorious view of the ocean and the sun-splashed terrace that looked perfect for leisurely mornings, she stood at the foot of the bed and pointed to a mangy-looking ring of twigs and feathers held together by rough thread. "This is our dream catcher," Susan explained. "It was made by a Native American artist. I had some of the feathers blessed by the Dalai Lama, the last time he gave a talk in New York. I'm *sure* this is the reason Honor always wakes up in a good mood." Honor, as we all knew, always shared her bed with her mother.

From the master bedroom window I saw the gorgeous pool in the garden below. The deck was lined with beautiful cobalt tiles.

"Handmade by Florentine artisans," Susan explained. A baby-safe teak fence surrounded the pool, which was covered in any case with a tarp.

We headed back downstairs, and Susan pointed to a wooden threshold. "The other half of the house is through those doors. There's a nice sitting room in there with one of the original fire-watercolors. It's where Harcourt has his office. He declared it a baby-free zone, so if you want to chill for a while, you can go in there. I never do."

The doors to Harcourt's preserve, I noticed, were graced with a double set of baby-proof locks.

"Susan, this place is perfect," I said, fantasizing about moving in permanently.

Susan made a face. "It wasn't easy getting it this way," she said. "I had to fight for it. I said to Harcourt, 'If you can buy yourself a new powerboat, I get my baby proofing!' Harcourt has such strong opinions on everything. Of course, that's what makes him so good at business. He's such a pioneer."

Despite the house's welcoming appearance, Susan was not entirely at ease in her Hamptons estate. "I've given the staff the weekend off," she confessed. On most days, she explained, there was the live-in caretaker, a full-time housekeeper, and a couple of Ecuadoran workmen who lived over the garage and who undertook various property maintenance projects as they arose. I could see that they all made her feel uncomfortable.

"I've told Harcourt I'd rather have a smaller place, something easier to maintain." She sighed. "I'd love to be able to do all my own gardening—I've always dreamed of growing organic vegetables. But Harcourt says it's important for his business to have a place that shows well."

Susan showed us each to our own room. As the token runaway, I was assigned the "aerie"—a self-contained upstairs suite decorated with silk toile wallpaper and a pair of original Audubon prints on either side of the double bed. I unpacked Anna, who had nodded off into her midafternoon nap, and lay on the bed next to her. I spent a few moments concentrating on my breath and doing my best to think of nothing at all. Then Anna woke, and I took her downstairs.

Susan was brewing a pot of tea made from some of the flowers in her garden. Nate was asleep next to Margaret, and the mamas were watching Honor move upright along the edge of the coffee table. "Look at that!" exclaimed Gigi approvingly. "She's very advanced!"

I placed Anna on the floor and she scurried over to the coffee table on her hands and knees. She pulled herself up and started walking next to Honor, using the table edge for support. Then, while Honor clung to the table, Anna released her hands and stood solo for the first time in her life. She looked around for encouragement.

"Wow!" Margaret said. "Now I'm impressed."

And she's two and half weeks younger than Honor! I thought, with a twinge of competitive pleasure.

Around dinnertime we lit up the barbecue. Isla ran to the local market for beef and swordfish steaks. Susan politely tried to ignore the slabs of dripping flesh—she had gone completely vegetarian after her pregnancy—and did her best to tempt us away from sin with offerings of stewed lentils and a salad. Trying to burnish my credentials as a good houseguest, I gamely sampled Susan's ascetic offerings first. The salad, which was actually quite good, tasted familiar to me. "I was inspired by the Le Refuge recipe," she said.

Ah, yes, I remembered—the Sacred Salad.

"It's such a shame that they don't let kids in. I'd love to be able to spend time there with Honor."

I nodded, then sneaked off to devour one of Gigi's juicy steaks.

The sun was setting, and most of the babies were winding down for the evening. One by one, the yoga mamas excused themselves to bathe their babies and tuck them into their beds. After I put Anna down, I sat on the terrace watching the stars come out like pinpricks of light in the darkening sky. The old, needling source of my distress emerged. So I grabbed my cell phone and called Mom. I told her about The Fight, about Le Refuge, and my new "aerie" in the Fielding house.

"You know this all has to end soon," she said.

"Mom, I'm having fun!"

"That's nice."

I got off the phone when the others joined me on the terrace. Margaret started grumbling again about Jonathan. "He's been calling me, just to 'talk.' The other day when he dropped Nate off, he asked if he could come in for a *cup of coffee!*" This, she seemed to suggest, was beyond the pale. "He's just trying to butter me up. Thinks I'll cut him a better deal. I'm going to talk with my lawyers about harassment."

In every other aspect of her life, Margaret was a paragon of functionality. But when she talked about Nate's father, I was starting to feel like she was losing her senses. She complained when he refused to talk to her, then complained twice as hard when he did. She said she wanted nothing to do with him, yet she grew indignant when he dated other women. And she insisted that Jonathan was a beast of a man, pure evil in the shape of a lawyer; but the man I saw playing with Nate on the swing set was no monster.

"Maybe you should hear what he has to say," I said tentatively. "When we met him in the park, he really seemed to care about Nate. Maybe he wants to be more involved? There might be another way of looking at the situation."

Margaret set her mouth in a grim line and said nothing.

Susan looked as though she wanted to add something, but she held back. She looked at me in a meaningful way. Then the phone rang, and she picked it up.

Jessica screeched so loudly I could hear her tinny voice from Susan's receiver. *"Oh my god, you're in the Hamptons this weekend! So are we!"*

Like a hound trailing the scent of money, Jessica had tracked Susan down.

Within minutes, Susan was cornered into accepting an invitation for brunch at Jessica's summer rental the next day. Isla rolled her eyes and Margaret shook her head in disgust, but Gigi was enthusiastic. "I like anyone who makes *me* look genteel," she joked after Susan had hung up. "Let's go over there and stir things up. And let's ask the guys if they want to come! I miss Charles and my Milton." Susan nodded vigorously. "Yes, let's invite the men. It would be wonderful to bring everyone together again."

With Harcourt perpetually AWOL, we all knew she meant only our men.

To my surprise, Isla supported the idea. "I cannot leave Azula in Antonio's hands any longer," she explained a little defensively. I figured there was more to it than that.

Susan turned to me. "You need to talk to Richard. It never hurts to talk."

I balked. Deep down, I knew she was right. It was the same advice I'd just given Margaret. But I was loath to call him. I didn't want him to think I would capitulate so easily. Then Gigi said, "Laura, call the guy, put him out of his misery. So maybe he's not perfect. But I've seen the way he looks at you. Like you're the sun and the moon."

I grudgingly took Gigi's proffered phone and dialed home. After four rings, the machine clicked on. Chagrined, I left a message. "I just want you to know that Anna's OK," I said. Gigi glared at me, so I added, "If you can break away from your bachelor life, maybe you could come up here." I gave him the details before hanging up. Susan announced she was ready for bed and went upstairs.

Gigi, who had opened her second bottle of wine while she thought no one was looking, decided to take her nightcap in her room. So Isla, Margaret, and I headed into the living room, as it was getting chilly outside. Isla seemed preoccupied. I wondered if she was thinking about John. She said she wanted to be by herself for a bit, and I watched as she wandered into Harcourt's preserve by herself.

A quarter of an hour passed. Margaret and I were flopped on the cushiony sofa, lazily flipping through some magazines and chatting sporadically. I started to wonder what Isla had found in Harcourt's part of the house. *What was she up to?* I poked my nose through the doors.

It felt like I was entering into an earlier era in the property's history. There were old trophies in the shape of tennis rackets and skis, antique furniture, and a fully stocked bar in the corner. On the wall behind the fireplace hung portraits and photographs of Harcourt's family line. Isla was sitting on an antique chair, a somber expression on her face. "What's wrong?" I asked. "I'm sure Azula is just fine."

She looked at me and shook her head. "No, it is not Azula."

She pointed to the wall of portraits, to the last of the line of Fielding ancestors. I glanced at the giant, black-and-white photograph of a handsome man, with deep-set eyes and distinguished, curly hair. Engraved on the frame was the name "J. Harcourt Fielding." It was clearly Susan's husband, the never-present Harcourt. As I stared at the image on the wall, the wheels of recognition slowly clicked into place. I looked at Isla in horror. "Isn't that . . ."

"John," she said, choking. "My John. Gigi's John."

Isla and I stared at the photograph for some time.

"My god, I have been such an idiot." Isla started laughing bitterly. "He is a very good liar, this John. I think he *believes* his lies. I think he is dangerous." She fell into silence again. We were both only starting to register the full implications of her discovery.

"I don't know what to believe anymore," I mumbled to myself.

Margaret poked her nose in.

She immediately sensed that everything was wrong.

"What is it?" she asked. Isla and I looked dumbly at the photo of J. Harcourt.

Margaret folded her arms. "I'm not leaving till you tell me what's wrong." She sounded stern but reassuring. I looked at Isla but she avoided my glance. "Susan's husband, Harcourt," I began, waving in the direction of the photo. I *wanted* to tell Margaret everything. I was sure she would know what to do. "He had an affair with . . ."

Isla looked at me sharply.

"Gigi," I finished the sentence, then looked back at Isla. But now she was looking at the ground.

Margaret looked incredulously from me to Isla.

"Really?"

"Yes," I said. The words came rushing out. I told Margaret the story of Gigi's whirlwind marriage, her earlier affair with John, and the fact that she believed that John was the father of her child. Then I turned to Isla. I was waiting for her to tell her part of the story. But Isla stayed silent.

"Are you absolutely sure it's John?" Margaret asked me, like she was cross-examining a reluctant witness.

"Of course I am!" I replied hotly. Isla nodded quietly.

Margaret paced for a few moments, tapping her fingers on her arm. "We have to show the picture to Gigi first," she announced. "*Then* we tell Susan."

I looked over at Isla, assuming she'd agree. But Isla hesitated. "Do we have to tell them? I mean, how is it necessary?" She faltered. "Maybe it will just hurt Susan even more. And what can Gigi do about it now anyway?"

Margaret set her mouth in a thin, tight line. "Gigi has to *confirm* that this is John. And she has a *right* to know who the father of her child is. This is a paternity case, for your information. And Susan has a right to know what her husband has been doing in his spare time."

Isla said nothing. I nodded, although I dreaded the prospect. At that moment, Gigi was certainly into her second bottle of wine, if not already dozing in an intoxicated stupor. We decided it would have to wait until morning. As we marched out of Harcourt's preserve and back into the rest of the house, headed for our bedrooms, I tried to catch Isla's eye. But she studiously avoided mine.

19

I don't really care what you believe. You should know
that by now. Belief is nothing! Belief is nothing.

—RODNEY YEE, *YOGA: THE POETRY OF THE BODY*

Gigi was snoring loudly. I wafted fresh coffee under her nose, to
no effect. I nudged her gently. Finally, I yanked hard on her legs.
"Fuck off, Milton!" she yelled, then rolled over and went back to
sleep. I went back downstairs to rejoin the others. Susan had got-
ten up early and baked us muffins from scratch for breakfast.

"The secret ingredient is seaweed!" she said cheerfully. "It
gives them a little kick, and it's healthy for all blood types!"

Isla handed Anna back to me, while Margaret held Nate and
pulled indifferently at her muffin. I found I was having a hard time
looking at Susan.

"What's up with Gigi?" Margaret said, giving me a searching look.

"She's not ready to face the world," I said grimly.

"Let her rest," Susan said. "We don't have to leave for Jessica's for another hour."

"By the way, Susan," Margaret said casually, "what's the 'J' for in J. Harcourt?"

Margaret was crossing the t's and dotting the i's in the legal brief in her mind.

"John. But he never uses it—except for official business. Half the men in his family are called John, so they always use middle names. Why do you ask?"

"Just wondering," Margaret mumbled.

Susan stirred a pot of nine-grain oatmeal for Honor, while Margaret and I tried to persuade our babies to eat little pieces of seaweed muffin. Anna threw hers down on the floor in disgust. An hour passed, and Gigi still hadn't joined us.

Susan began packing up extra diapers and snacks for the kids and prepared to load up the car. "I promised Jessica we'd come by on the early side," she said apologetically. Margaret motioned to Isla and me to keep an eye on Nate. She climbed the stairs. "Fuck you, Milton!" we heard Gigi say. And then, in a groggy voice, "Oh, hey, hon, I'm sorry, thanks for waking me up. Am I late?"

By the time Gigi showered, dressed, and made it downstairs, Susan had already packed her daughter and our gear in Isla's Hummer and was waiting for us to get the show on the road. "Come on, let's do it. Now!" Margaret whispered to Isla and me urgently. "We will be there in a minute," Isla called out to Susan, who was hovering around in the car in the driveway. We approached Gigi, who was eyeing one of the muffins suspiciously. "Gigi," I said. "I want to show you something." I picked up Anna and Margaret grabbed Nate, then we guided her toward Harcourt's preserve. She raised her eyebrows. "Screw the no-baby rule!" Margaret said, by way of explanation. We maneuvered her in front of Harcourt's photograph. "Do you know this man?" Margaret asked. Gigi blinked her eyes and let out a gasp of recognition.

"It's John," she whispered, glancing at me. "What's his picture doing here?"

"This is Susan's husband, Harcourt," I said, reluctantly.

Gigi stood mutely for a few moments, fully absorbing the shock. Then she started shaking her head. "That bastard!" she said. "He never told me he was *married!*" Then she turned to me, wide-eyed. "What if he is . . . ? What if Charles is . . . ? Oh my god, what about *Susan?* Does Susan know?"

I shook my head. "Susan doesn't have a clue."

"What have I done?" Gigi sobbed.

Then she looked at Margaret. "How do *you* know about John?"

"I only found out last night," Margaret volunteered limply.

"I . . . we saw the photo last night," I stuttered. "We had to tell Margaret."

Isla nodded silently.

Margaret added, "Nobody else knows. Laura, Isla, and me, we just want to help you—and Susan."

Gigi collapsed back into an armchair. "Poor Susan. She doesn't deserve this. Oh, Charles, my Charles . . ."

"We're ready!" Susan shouted impatiently from the driveway.

"You go," Margaret turned to Isla. "See if you can stall her." Isla nodded and went off to her car, where Susan was waiting. Gigi was still slumped in her chair. "That lying scum," she kept repeating.

"We need to talk to Susan," Margaret announced. "I need to see her prenup."

Gigi sat up. She pointed at the large mahogany desk in front of her. "Is this Harcourt's desk?" she asked.

I nodded. "It must be."

She started pulling at the drawers. They were locked. She grabbed a letter opener from the desk and began to fiddle with the locks. Margaret and I looked at her with surprise. "Something my daddy taught me," she snarled.

I heard a sharp click.

"Bingo." Gigi smiled and heaved the top drawer open.

It flew out, showering a trail of papers. Placing Anna on the floor beside me, I bent down next to Margaret and hurriedly began to collect them. My greedy eyeballs scanned the contents of utility bills, insurance forms, and house title deeds. Then I saw a sheaf of papers on Dr. Bruce's stationery. I took a close look. It was a massive bill addressed to Harcourt. Over the calendar month of June, Dr. Bruce claimed 100 hours of therapy for "Mrs. Susan Fielding," and he charged a whopping $400 per hour. The total came to $40,000.

Four hundred dollars an hour? It seemed like a ridiculous amount for any therapist to charge. But more to the point, I realized that Susan could not have spent 100 hours on Dr. Bruce's couch in the space of a single month. One hundred hours worked out to *five hours* every weekday. I showed the papers to Margaret.

"This is fraud," she said, her eyes widening. Then she shuffled the papers underneath the bill. "Or maybe it's worse. . . ." she said, her voice faltering.

Underneath the bill were pages of notes.

June 10. The patient continues to resist the suggestion that she has a severe, clinical condition. The patient resists electroshock therapy treatment. The patient resists in-patient treatment at a psychiatric facility.

June 17. The patient shows no interest in altering her current family arrangements. She resists the suggestion that her daughter may be too difficult for her to handle. The patient does, however, respond favorably to the suggestion that money may be at the source of her troubles.

June 24. Patient refuses to take antidepressants on grounds that she is breastfeeding. Will continue to advise.

We looked at each other.

"It's entirely unethical for Dr. Bruce to pass on his notes to Harcourt," Margaret said, sounding uncharacteristically flustered.

I found a folder marked "confidential" and handed it to Margaret. "This is from a firm of private investigators," she said, glancing briefly at the contents.

"*Schwing!*" Gigi shouted. She was on her hands and knees, the epicenter of a small explosion of papers. She handed a binder to Margaret. "The prenup," she announced.

Margaret scanned the document for a few moments, quickly flipping through its pages. About halfway through, she stopped to examine a passage. "It says here that if Harcourt can prove that Susan is psychologically unfit to be a mother, he can divorce her and pay her nothing," she stated flatly. "That's why he's got that therapist."

We heard Susan's voice from the driveway again. "Can I help you guys with something?"

"Let me go to see what they are doing," we heard Isla saying.

Margaret looked at me. "You go with them to Jessica's. Tell Susan that Gigi and I will follow in Gigi's car in a few minutes."

I balanced Anna on my hip and rushed to the door, leaving Gigi, Margaret, and Nate surrounded by papers. Susan was just coming back into the house, with Isla fretting behind her, when I made it to the threshold.

"Ready?" Susan said, smiling as we almost bumped into each other.

"Let's go," I said, trying to smile back.

20

Let me tell you, the Joneses are very
messed-up people!

—BARON BAPTISTE, *JOURNEY INTO POWER*

Jessica's rental was a three-bedroom contemporary located a few streets in from the beach. The décor looked as though it had been lifted from a Midtown hotel—paintings of oceans and sunsets, wooden ducks hanging on the walls, an elaborate fireplace that seemed distinctly out of place on a sweltering summer day. The coffee tables sagged under piles of magazines—*Vanity Fair, Town & Country, W.* The pool was a forlorn rectangle of blue in the otherwise empty front lawn. It was the kind of house that could be had for "only $120,000" for the season, as Jessica repeatedly informed us.

It was *not* the kind of house designed with toddlers in mind. The split-level plan meant that there were steps everywhere—from the entryway to the living room, from the living room to the kitchen, from the kitchen to the dining room. The open staircase had a single banister that rode on only a handful of struts—leaving gaps more than large enough for a tot to fall through. The front porch area had no fence. The pool had no tarp—there was nothing between baby and the bottom but three feet of shimmering blue water.

Jessica gave us the tour along with several other guests who had arrived late. "We're in the market," she offered by way of apology for her humble rental, "but we're testing the waters before buying. We want to try out different neighborhoods and see which one we like best."

A petite woman in a sleeveless flowered dress and a large sun hat nodded. "You guys picked a great spot. I just love the way you can hear the ocean," she said.

I strained to hear the ocean, too, and concluded that what we were hearing was the noise of the nearby roadway.

"Thanks," said Jessica. "But we could use more space. Next year we're going to rent a five-bedroom. Steve says you can get one for the season for only one hundred seventy-five K."

The woman nodded appreciatively.

Margaret rolled her eyes at me impatiently.

We found Susan in the windowless children's play area with Honor, Cameron, and Jessica's nanny. She was a new nanny, I could see, but she looked just as bored and unhappy as the previous one. Jessica's plan was to dump all the kids with the nanny and take the adults and the party outdoors. But when Jessica had suggested Susan put Honor with the nanny, Susan brought her in and stayed there herself. I could see the small camera eye in the corner of the playroom. I mugged for the "nannycam," in case Steve was looking.

Margaret and I put our charges down on the floor to let them stretch. We all felt that we couldn't leave Susan inside on her own, so we stayed with her in the play area while Jessica led the rest of her guests outside. "Don't go, mommy," whimpered a toddler in neat pigtails. *"Maman,"* the woman corrected her. From her accent, it sounded like she was from Nebraska. "Don't worry, we have a nannycam screen by the pool," Jessica reassured her on their way out. The nanny's eyes narrowed grimly. "We'll join you in a minute," Gigi called after them. She was wearing hangover attire: a big hat and dark sunglasses.

The children's play area quickly descended into chaos. With so many lethal or breakable objects within easy reach, we couldn't relax. The little ones soon tired of hearing "no" and delivered their verdict in the form of chain screams: First one would cry, then another, until the whole house was shaking.

"Well, that does it for me!" Gigi said. "I need some fresh air."

"Go ahead!" Susan said cheerfully. "You too," she added, looking at Margaret and me. "Nicolette and I will watch the kids."

I could tell that Margaret was just as desperate to get out as I was. "There's nothing we can do in here," she whispered to me, glancing in between the nanny and the nannycam.

As we came back outside to the pool area, Gigi sniffled.

"Are you feeling all right?" Jessica said, with false concern.

"Fine, fine, think I'll sit down," Gigi mumbled, gesturing toward the lawn chairs. "Anything to drink?" she added sharply.

"Of course," said Jessica, pointing Gigi in the direction of a table near the pool laden with pitchers of lemonade and sangria.

As the afternoon wore on, and it seemed certain that Richard would not show, I admitted to myself that I genuinely missed him. With the trauma of the past day, some of my wrath now seemed misplaced. And despite all my complaints about his parenting skills, I longed for my old best friend and confidant. I wanted to tell him everything. But the party was already three hours old, and there was no sign of *any* of the yoga papas. *Why hadn't Richard called back? Where was he?*

I wandered on the grass by the pool, toward the bar. I poured myself a tall glass of sangria. It was the first time I had had more than a sip or two of alcohol since I'd found out I was pregnant. The resulting buzz made me feel slightly guilty—I knew that alcohol would make its way into my breast milk—but it gave me a temporary sense of relief.

Feeling fuzzy inside, I rubbed the grass under my fingers. I glanced over at the nannycam screen for the twentieth time. Susan was doing her best to cheer up the tots, but I could see that they hated Jessica's play area just as much as the nanny did. Emboldened by the sangria, I marched back inside and waved Margaret along with me. "I'm taking Anna out into the sun," I announced when we got to the play area. "Anyone care to join me?"

Jessica's nanny shook her head, unwilling to break the house rules. Susan looked as if she wanted to join us, but politely stayed with the nanny. Margaret and I grabbed our unhappy tots and took them out anyway.

Anna and Nate trilled with relief as we laid them on towels on the grass. Jessica shot us a sour look, but we ignored her. Soon everyone's attention was distracted by the sound of a car pulling into the driveway. To my astonishment, it was a Cheetah—a bright red, marriage-wrecking Cheetah from Amalgamated Motors. To my even greater astonishment, *Richard* was hopping out of the driver's seat.

I felt a lump in my throat. I wanted to punish him for his tardiness, for ruining my weekend, for failing me as a coparent, for driving a . . . Cheetah?! And I wanted to hug him, tell him how much I missed him, tell him about how Anna had stood up without holding the coffee table. In short, I didn't know what I wanted to do, so I just stood there in an alcoholic haze.

Richard walked up to me looking annoyingly pleased with himself. "Hey, what do you think of this car?" he asked, oblivious to my inner turmoil.

"Aren't you going to say you're happy to see us?" I demanded.

He stiffened and let out a sigh. Behind me, out of our view, Anna had propped herself on a lawn chair into a standing position.

"After you've taken our baby and run out of the house, I'm not sure," he replied.

It was not what I needed to hear.

"You . . . you're blaming *me?*"

Another car rumbled into the driveway, an ordinary sedan. Antonio climbed out of the driver's seat and pulled Azula from the backseat. Milton got out of the other side of the car and retrieved Charles. Antonio grinned hello, oblivious to the crackling tension between my husband and me. On his way over to Isla, he slapped Richard on the back and said, "Hey, thanks, Richie."

Richard, who in fact hated being called Richie, turned aside from our brewing argument long enough to reply, "It was awesome!"

The moment Isla got a good look at Azula, she shrieked. "She is filthy!"

"Come on, honey, it's just a little ketchup," said Antonio.

"*Ketchup!* What did you feed her?!"

"A hot dog."

Isla shrieked again. "You do not know that babies can choke on hot dogs and die? Do you not listen to nothing?!"

Meanwhile, Milton had ambled up to Gigi with Charles in his arms. Gigi remained in her lawn chair, with sunglasses over her eyes and a glass of sangria in her hand. "Hey, hon, so glad you came to see me," she slurred affectionately. Milton's mouth tightened and he gripped his son. Disappointment mixed with disgust on his face as he took in the line of empty glasses around Gigi's chair. "For chrissake, Geeg, can't you take one afternoon off?"

"Ducky, please," she said. "Cut me a break just this once. Just today."

"Yeah, today is special, just like yesterday, and the day before, and the day before," he said, his voice choppy.

While Antonio and Isla argued about the state of Azula's hygiene and Milton and Gigi argued about Gigi's drinking, Richard and I simply argued, flat out. I was shouting, "I did not run away! You drove me out! Besides, I tried to call you!" Richard bellowed back, "What are you talking about, you self-dramatizing lunatic? You walked out! You left a message saying you were 'seeking refuge'! What the hell is that?"

"You act like you're the fucking king of the castle and I'm your servant!"

"*What?*"

While Richard and I were bickering, Anna let go of the lawn chair and took her first step. And then her second. She was walking. Not yet eleven months old, Anna had rightfully earned the proud name of "toddler." She started to toddle across the grass.

"Look at this," Isla screeched as if she had found a tarantula crawling on her daughter. She leaned over and sniffed Azula's shirt. "I thought so!" she announced with vicious triumph. "Olive oil. You took her to the bar!"

Antonio held out his hands helplessly. "So what?"

"*So what?* You took her to Extra Virgin so all the girls could fuss over you and play mommy!" Isla was in a rage.

"Everybody loved her! She had a great time!"

Isla twisted her daughter out of Antonio's hands.

Gigi leaned up from her lawn chair and reached for her baby. Milton pulled Charles away. "I don't want him to smell your breath," he said tensely.

Gigi started to cry.

Anna reached the cement skirt surrounding the pool. The cement stood about an inch off the grass. She strode onto the pool platform like an actress stepping onto a stage for her curtain call.

"You ruined our weekend at Le Refuge," I wailed. "You wrecked my chances for a third Shirodhara-Ayurvedic Fusion Journey!"

Richard looked confused. "I was trying to reach out to you—"

"By telling them that I had a *baby?*"

Another car rolled up the driveway. It was Jonathan. In the back of my mind, it clicked: Susan must have invited Jonathan on the sly last night, after she had supposedly gone to bed. She had held on to his card from when we met in the playground. She was such a romantic. Margaret's mouth dropped a fraction of an inch, then slammed shut. "What are *you* doing here?" she growled.

"Well, uh, I heard that—"

"Take it up with my lawyer!" Margaret said fiercely.

"Hey, I'm just trying to say hello?"

"I'm not doing anything extrajudicial!"

"Would you calm down for a minute, Margaret? You seem kind of stressed."

"Excuse me, Jonathan, if I *am* stressed. I have a baby to take care of without any help from its fucking father!"

"Hey, don't swear in front of our boy!"

"Who are you now, Miss fucking Manners?"

Over on the other side of the lawn, Isla was shouting. "And why did you buy that stupid car? Do you plan to drive off to California with one of your twenty-two-year-old girlfriends? I *know* which one it is, by the way! How did I end up picking such a shit-sucking worm?"

"Easy, bitch!" Antonio yelled back.

"Richard, you didn't have to tell Le Refuge about the baby!" I screamed at my husband.

"You weren't registered in your name! I just asked for the woman with the baby!"

"How did you even know we were at Le Refuge anyway?!"

"Your mom told me."

"So why did you call me anyway?" I asked, my attack faltering.

Anna reached the side of the pool. She curled her tiny toes around the edge. She tilted her head forward and gazed, mezmerized, at her reflection.

"Please, please let me have my baby," Gigi said in a rush of slurry sobs.

"You are like gangrene, I should cut you off!" Isla screamed.

"I wouldn't be suing you if you had done your part, asshole!" Margaret roared.

"I called you at Le Refuge because I wanted to send you flowers!"

I looked at Richard dumbly. Then I heard a faint splash.

I turned toward the pool and saw my beautiful daughter's head submerge in the clear blue water.

21

Truth alone conquers.

—*THE MUNDAKA UPANISHAD*

Parenting is often simply the art of relaxing and watching the miracle happen. Give them milk and love, and babies will learn to sit up, flip over, crawl, and walk—pretty much on their own. Sing them the ABCs while they fuss and ignore you, and then one day, without warning, they'll sing the whole alphabet back to you. And, if you should throw one of these remarkable babies into deep water, they will sometimes exhibit an innate swimming reflex.

Other times they will take a large gulp of water and drown.

There are no guarantees.

The next thing I remember was Anna splashing water in my face with her flailing arms, coughing and crying with gusto. Richard held us both in his arms at the shallow end of the pool. Jonathan was in the water next to us. So were Antonio, Margaret, and Milton, all wearing their lawn-party clothes. On the grass nearby, the other mamas and babies were watching us, calling out to confirm that Anna was fine. I found myself unable to speak, except in squawks. Anna spluttered and looked at me.

"Ma," she said.

And she let out an impish grin.

I cried with joy, my tears mixing with the water from the pool. I held my baby tight. When I finally recovered the power of speech, I whispered to her, "I'm never going to let you go." Richard squeezed both of us. "Laura, Anna, I love you so much." To my surprise, I saw that some of the water streaking down his face wasn't coming from his dripping hair. When Richard at last pried Anna from my grip, he held her up to announce, "She walks! She swims! She talks!"

Everybody clambered out of the pool, clothes dripping with water. Jessica was flapping around anxiously saying, "This is *precisely* why I don't allow children outside," to anybody who would listen.

I kicked off my soaking sandals and ran to my husband and precious baby. As we lay together on Jessica's front lawn, breathing in the fragrant summer air and gazing up into the cloudless sky, it was hard to remember why I ever lost faith in my beautiful husband. My frustration with his sloppiness, the unequal division of labor, his deciding to learn ancient Greek receded for the moment. A small voice told me that we would soon be fighting over the dishes and laundry, and I would have to storm out of the house a few more times. But a stronger, richer voice told me that I would always come home. Richard nipped my neck. "I was so lonely without you," he said.

I sighed. "I thought you wouldn't notice I left until you ran out of clean socks."

Richard gave me the ironic smile he used to use, long ago, when we were sharing an inside joke. "You're the fabric softener of my life, you're my bleach, you're everything."

Not the compliment a woman spends a lifetime waiting for, but I took it.

"Richard," I said, "please, let's be partners. I mean, *real* partners. With Anna, with us. Don't leave it all to me."

Richard smiled. "I'll try. I promise I'll try."

And while I wasn't sure I believed him—I took that too.

I laughed, and we embraced again. We wrapped the towel around ourselves and rolled around on the grass like a giant family burrito. We came to a halt in front of Jonathan and Margaret, who were sitting on the grass cross-legged, soaking, with baby Nate in between them. They were eyeing each other quietly, sullen and suspicious, unsure what to say.

Susan came over to them carrying an armload of Jonathan's possessions. In his mad dash into the pool, Jonathan had dropped his bag, scattering its contents across the lawn. In her hand, Susan held forward a wallet-sized leather booklet that belonged to him. She sat down next to Margaret and Jonathan and opened it for all to see. It was a miniature photo album—a brag book.

As we watched mutely, Susan flipped through the photos. Mostly, they were pictures of Nate, or of Nate and Jonathan. A couple of them included parts of Jonathan's face and forearm—he had obviously taken the pictures himself. At the end were two shots of Margaret—one a casual snapshot of her standing with several other colleagues, looking at the camera and wearing a quizzical expression. The other was a close-up of Margaret's face, eyes closed, asleep, her mouth parted in a gentle smile. On the edge of the frame I could see part of a laptop keyboard and a legal pad. Jonathan must have taken the photo surreptitiously as she napped at the office.

Jonathan turned red and looked at the ground. Margaret's mouth dropped wide open. She suddenly looked helpless, almost frightened. I realized then just how vulnerable she was at heart, how hard it had been for someone who had always thought of herself as a plain girl from the vanilla suburbs of New York to believe that anyone could really love her. For probably the first time in her life, Margaret was speechless. Then she turned to Jonathan. "Why didn't you tell me?" she stammered. "Why did you . . . ?" She trailed off. Jonathan leaned over and gave her a hug. "Come on, Margaret, you were suing me. Can't we start over?"

A smile blossomed across Margaret's face, the kind of wide, elated smile I had seen on her when we'd visited the fateful place where she and Jonathan had shared their last, happy moment.

She put her hand on Jonathan's. "I . . . well, OK, *maybe*," she said.

We pulled back a few feet, to let Jonathan and Margaret rediscover each other after such a long stretch in their legal fortresses.

"I knew they were in love," insisted Gigi. She turned to Susan and whispered, "You are a genius."

"I . . . I just want everyone to be as happy as Harcourt and myself," Susan stammered.

Gigi gave Susan a look of pity. I exchanged glances with Margaret and Isla. It was time. I put my hand on Richard's shoulder. "There's something we need to do. Can you take Anna into the house? You too, Jonathan, Milton, Antonio. Watch the babies for us."

Jessica showed the menfolk inside. The few remaining party guests who had been gawking at us since the pool debacle all understood that this was their cue to leave.

The yoga mamas gathered in a circle on the far corner of the lawn. Susan looked confused. Honor had crawled up into her lap and fallen asleep, and Susan stroked her hair gently, as though soothing herself. "Susan," Margaret started. "We need to tell you something."

Susan kept stroking Honor.

"Your husband is planning to force you out of your marriage. He is using Dr. Bruce to get you declared psychologically unfit to be a mother."

"That's not true," Susan said, bewildered. "Dr. Bruce is trying to help me."

"No," Margaret said firmly. "Harcourt wants to get you out, and he is counting on the prenup to let him do it. Your prenup entitles him to divorce you and pay you essentially nothing if he can show that you are psychologically unfit to be a mother."

"But Harcourt would *never*," Susan said, trembling. In her voice I heard doubt and denial jumbled together.

"We've seen the evidence," I added.

"No, you don't understand, you don't know what you're talking about—"

"We also found reports from a private investigator," Margaret continued. "He had one trailing you, just in case you did anything that he could use against you in court. You remember the guy who spooked us when we went shopping last Christmas?"

"But you said he was after *you*," Susan said.

"I was wrong." Margaret paused, and looked momentarily distracted. Then she regained her focus and continued speaking. "If Harcourt gets you declared unfit to be a mother, he won't just divorce you and leave you penniless. He might take Honor with him."

Susan clutched her sleeping baby, refusing to look at Margaret. Denial was winning the day.

"Honey, we're gonna stop him," Gigi blurted. "There's something I need to tell you," she said. "It's about Harcourt."

Susan stiffened. "Oh, it's OK. I'm . . . he's going to call. He'll come here sometime, maybe next week."

Gigi lunged forward and gave Susan a violent hug. "Sugar," she said, "I had an affair with your husband. Before I met you. Before I met my Milton! Hon, he didn't tell me he was married. He said his name was John."

Susan closed her eyes.

"We always had to meet in secret. I should have known! And I'm pretty sure I wasn't his first."

Susan shook her head tightly back and forth and frown lines appeared on either side of her mouth. "No," she said, in an agitated voice. "There must be some mistake, a lot of people look alike," she said, her eyes darting around to each of us. She was trembling.

"Susan, do you think I would ever, *ever* jeopardize my Charles's future?"

Susan looked uncertain. "No . . ."

Gigi broke down in tears. "I think Harcourt is the father of my child."

Susan gave her a strange look, almost a smile.

"I'm gonna have a paternity test," Gigi sobbed. "That will *prove* Harcourt cheated on you. Won't it, Margaret?"

Margaret put her hand on Gigi's shoulder. "It might, Gigi." She turned to Susan. "Your prenup entitles you to divorce Harcourt and keep your share of the assets—and Honor—if you can demonstrate in court that he was unfaithful."

Susan ignored Margaret, reached over to Gigi and brushed her hair back. "Don't worry," she said, clear and firm. "Harcourt isn't the father of your child."

"I'm telling you he *is*."

"No. He can't be."

"He *can* be, that's the problem!" Gigi shrieked, desperate that she wasn't getting through to Susan. "I'm telling you, we had an *affair*. I—"

"I believe you," Susan interrupted. She suddenly seemed in control, as though she had known everything all along. "Harcourt can't be the father of your child." She paused. "Harcourt is infertile. He has a condition called azoospermia," she continued. "In his case, it's untreatable. I tried to get pregnant with him for years before he finally saw a doctor and we figured it out."

A wave of relief washed across Gigi's face. "But what about Honor?" she asked.

"Honor is my own," Susan said self-consciously. "I used a sperm donor. Donor number one-eight-seven," she added with a faint smile. "I never told anyone because Harcourt . . ." Susan sighed.

We all stayed quiet for a few moments.

"This makes our case a little tougher," Margaret announced, glumly. "It means we'd have to rely on Gigi's testimony, instead of DNA evidence."

I looked sharply at Isla. She looked back at me silently.

Gigi looked up defiantly. "I don't care. I need to save our Susan. I could do it."

Margaret looked somber, and her voice was steel. "These things are never easy, especially when you're up against an adversary as rich and well connected as Harcourt. It would mean agreeing to testify in court. It would mean putting your entire past up for display, having every one of your secrets picked apart by a vicious lawyer."

"I'm gonna stop him!" Gigi blurted out. "I'm gonna stand up there in court and tell the whole damn world that he cheated on you with me. I don't care if everybody knows. That's the way to stop him, right, Margaret?"

"But, Gigi," Susan said softly, "you can't do that. Milton will never forgive you."

I looked again at Isla. But still she sat quietly, taking in everything with her dark and melancholy eyes.

"She's right," Margaret said. "They'll try to crucify you on the stand. They'll challenge your credibility on every point. Dredge up family history, bring in your brother from rehab, call all your old boyfriends. They'll know that the two of you are friends. They might argue that you cut a deal, that Gigi has a stake in your settlement." She nodded to Susan. "And if they succeed in making Gigi seem even the slightest bit unreliable, our case falls apart."

"I don't care what they think," Gigi said, tears welling up in her eyes. "You're my friend, Susan, you and the rest of you yoga mamas are——"

Isla cleared her throat. "You do not need to go in front of the lawyers," she said firmly to Gigi. She looked around at the rest of us. "I have a much better plan."

22

The person who practices yoga regularly will not become a victim but a master of his or her circumstances and time.

—B.K.S. IYENGAR, *YOGA: THE PATH TO HOLISTIC HEALTH*

"Oh, John, I am so glad you understand me."

Isla looked up at us with a fraught expression. Her lip quivered a little, but otherwise her performance was magnificent. "Yes, I came by myself to relax. I needed time alone away from Antonio, but now . . . You would? I'm in the Honeymoon Chalet at Le Refuge—you know it?" She gave us a thumbs-up. "What time does your helicopter arrive?" Isla hung up the phone, purring, "I'll be waiting here for you at nine P.M."

"Awesome!" Margaret said.

Isla wrinkled up her perfect nose. "I feel like I need a shower."

Gigi looked hurt. It was clear she still wasn't sure what to make of Isla's affair. "That guy's got some brass balls," she marveled to Susan. "He tells you he's on a business trip, and then he comes up to the Hamptons to screw some other broad."

Isla stared at the floor. Susan grimaced and looked ready to cry.

"OK, girls, let's get to work!" Margaret snapped.

Getting back into Le Refuge had been the trickiest part of the plan.

We approached the Spa Lady mournfully and overwhelmed her with our apologies. We said we'd learned from our mistakes, pleaded with her to give us another chance, and offered double the chalet's nightly rate. We even invited her to inspect our car and bags as proof that we were bringing no babies or foreign substances onto the sacred grounds of Le Refuge. Of course, we were careful to stash our two bottles of champagne in the bushes before the Spa Lady performed her inspection. We were in fact clean on the baby issue. We had left our children in the care of our men at Jessica's place. Since the men owed us some child-care time and Jessica was willing to do anything Susan asked, no one had objected.

After she'd poked her nose in Antonio's car—the giant black Hummer—Spa Lady at last relented. "Sometimes it takes time to find spiritual balance," she allowed, suggesting that our earlier misbehavior could be excused as the consequence of the unbelievably bad *chi* emanating from Manhattan.

"We are only here to seek the truth," Susan said reverently.

Once inside the chalet, we unpacked Jessica's "nannycam" surveillance system—two laptops, a wireless networking base station, and a digital video camera. "Borrowing" the system had been a cinch. As Susan had discovered during her grueling hours in Jessica's play area, Jessica's new nanny was fed up with her boss. We slipped her a big tip and she happily looked the other way.

While Isla, Susan, and I got the spyware up and running, Margaret and Gigi scouted around the master bedroom at the rear of Honeymoon Chalet in search of the best place to hide the camera. They found the perfect spot: a cabinet in the corner with a bizarre, multilevel flowerpot on top. We hid the laptop in the cabinet and ran a cord up to the camera, which Margaret nestled gently among the flowers. Unless one knew where to look for it, the system would be invisible. Then, we got the wireless network up and running between the two laptops. I logged in from the second laptop and, to my delight, was able to view the camera images and pick up sound through the network.

"Ka-ching!" Gigi said appreciatively.

"Let's make sure this works from the parking lot," I said.

Our plan was to lie low in the parking lot and keep tabs on Isla through the network connection. The camera was loaded with digital tape, which we figured would give us all the evidence we needed. Isla's code word was "Shirodhara." That was the word that would bring us crashing back into the Honeymoon Chalet to pull the plug on Harcourt's evil schemes.

Susan, Gigi, and I went out to the Hummer and powered up the laptop through the car's cigarette lighter. We saw Margaret smiling at us on the screen through the camera in the master bedroom. "Testing one-two-three," I heard her say through the laptop's tinny speakers. Isla stood nervously in the background.

At 8:30 P.M., as it was getting dark, we took up positions. Margaret, Gigi, Susan, and I climbed into the rear area of the car, with the backseat down. I put the laptop up against the back of the front seat. We could see Isla lying on the bed in a silk bathrobe. Next to her, a couple of bottles of champagne sweated in an ice bucket. Underneath the robe she was wearing an elaborate bathing suit that looked like a series of black ace bandages wrapped around her long, lean torso at various alluring angles.

"It's almost impossible to take off," she assured us. "Last time I tried, I needed two assistants."

On any other woman, such a high-concept swimsuit would have looked silly. On Isla, it was a scintillating combination of fashion and fetish.

A tense forty-five minutes passed. We whispered to each other in the back of the Hummer, even though nobody could hear us. In the chalet, Isla paced the room nervously or flopped down on the bed and flipped listlessly through magazines. On the nannycam screen, some strange icons appeared, but since they didn't interfere with the system, I ignored them.

Then we saw headlights. A taxi. We ducked. We heard the taxi door slam. I peeked out the car window. A tall man with curly hair in a dark suit stood on the driveway and looked toward the chalet, a bouquet of roses tucked under his arm. He wore a self-satisfied grin. Susan peeked out alongside me. She gave me a sad, thin smile. Tears welled up in her clear blue eyes. Sure enough, it was Harcourt.

He headed straight for the door of the Honeymoon Chalet. He

knocked playfully, and when Isla answered the door he proffered the flowers before stepping inside.

A nerve-wracking ten minutes passed before Isla maneuvered Harcourt within microphone range of the camera in the master bedroom. I wondered if she was deliberately sparing Susan the inevitable intimacy of their greeting.

"Pour me a glass," we finally heard Isla saying as she came onto our screen.

Harcourt reached over and popped open one of the bottles of champagne.

"So what made you come out here?" he asked.

"I needed time off," Isla said, as Harcourt poured. "I want to try some new things."

"New things," he said, raising his eyebrows suggestively.

"Yes! New things," Isla purred, leaning into him and then pulling away teasingly. "My relationship with Antonio is so boring. I don't think we're meant to spend every minute with the same person for the rest of our lives. Do you?"

Harcourt guffawed and gulped down his champagne. "'Course not."

While he was concentrating on his drink, Isla, as we could see, surreptitiously emptied her glass into one of the waiting flowerpots.

"Good girl," Gigi mumbled.

"Don't you agree with me?" Isla pressed.

"Of course I do," Harcourt replied pompously. "From an evolutionary point of view, it doesn't make any sense. Our drives are what they are—we can't override them. Biology is destiny." He looked at Isla with curiosity. "You know, you're amazing. Most women don't understand these things. They're too sentimental. But you—" He moved in closer to her. "We have a lot in common, you and me."

She held him off by holding out her empty glass. He poured for both.

Again he gulped it down, and she got another plant inebriated. Refilling their glasses again, she emptied out the bottle.

"Wow, you're something special." He grinned. He reached over and brushed his hand against a knee peeping through her bathrobe.

She smiled demurely and pulled back. "Me? You are the special one, I am sure. You never talk about your past, but a guy like you, there *must* be so many . . ." She put on a petulant expression. "Sometimes I think the people who are the single ones do not understand. You do not know what it is like to be in a marriage prison and to feel like you cannot breathe. You may think that you know what it is like but unless you *live* it—"

"Hey, I'm not single either," Harcourt blurted. "I mean, we have a similar arrangement. I do my thing, she does hers. Just like you and, uh—"

"Antonio," Isla completed his sentence with a mischievous smile. "So does it mean I am a part of your 'secret life'?"

Harcourt growled as he moved in closer. "Yes, you're my little secret!"

Isla pulled back and tried again. "Oooh, tell me about your other little secrets. I *love* to hear sexy stories." She put on a mock frown. "Or am I the only one who has these stories?"

"Oh, I've got lots of stories," Harcourt said.

Isla looked at him as though he'd just announced he'd won the World's Best Lover contest. "John, I am hearing a new side of you," she flirted. "I want to be, how do you say, kinky. I want to listen to your stories. You have never told them to me. Now you must tell me everything!" As a form of enticement, she slipped her robe down over her arms, revealing her fabulously complicated bathing suit. Harcourt swallowed hard.

"That's some lingerie," he commented.

"Adventures!" Isla pouted.

"Well, I travel a lot on business," he began.

"So you make sex with women from all over the world?"

"Of course!" Harcourt smiled. "I'm very international!"

Isla began to tease out the details of Harcourt's sordid past. He started to list women he had slept with, city by city, describing luxurious hotel suites, lingerie, and sexual practices, while Isla alternately cooed in admiration of his prowess and gagged into the camera for our benefit. Gigi made the list: "Then there was this chick from Queens. She talked like Tony Soprano in tights. But she could screw all day!"

"This is great stuff!" Margaret whispered, scribbling notes in the back of the Hummer.

"The son of a bitch," said Gigi.

All the talk was clearly starting to make Harcourt a little restless. "C'mon, babe, what's with all the chatter tonight?" he said, taking off his tie. He reached over and caressed Isla's thigh.

She fended him off again with her champagne glass. "Oops—empty!" she said coyly. "I will be back to you in a minute," she said, moving off into the bathroom as Harcourt popped the second bottle of champagne and poured.

While she was in the bathroom, Harcourt sat down on an armchair and took off his shoes.

Isla returned and lay down on the bed.

"So, is there anybody you haven't slept with?" She was starting to sound a little sarcastic.

"Oh, yeah. There's this skanky blond with a hard ass; she's practically offering a menu of services if I'll help her kid get into preschool."

"Her name?" Isla asked, incredulous.

"Jessica."

Suddenly our laptop screen filled up with the face of a man in a business suit. Jessica's husband, Steve!

"What the——? *Who the hell are you?*" he shouted through the tinny loudspeakers of our laptop.

"Crap!" Margaret said to me. "Nobody told me about Internet accessibility! He must have found us through the hotel's wireless network!"

"Sorry!" I said, while Margaret furiously worked the keyboard to block Steve from the network.

"Now there's one unhappy hubby!" Gigi roared from the backseat.

When Margaret got the picture back on Isla, we could see that Harcourt had unbuttoned his shirt.

"Are we being kinky?" She fluttered her eyes coquettishly.

"Very, very kinky!" Harcourt responded, draining his glass and making a move to get out of his chair.

"Am I the best lover of all these other women?" Isla asked.

"The best." Harcourt stood up and leaned over the bed.

"Really the best?"

"Yes, you are fantastic."

Isla rolled over like a kitten. "John, I have an idea."

"Tell me."

"I want to watch you take off your clothes. Put on a show for me."

"Huh?"

"Take off your clothes—but take them off very slowly," she said, lying back on the bed. She lifted up one leg, revealing the inside of her thigh. "And maybe we could use some of this," Isla said, pulling out a bottle of Extra Virgin Sauce.

"Yeah!" Harcourt growled, standing at the foot of the bed.

I kept my eyes glued to the screen, ready to leap out of the car at a moment's notice.

Harcourt took off his cufflinks, swaying and making striptease trumpet sounds.

As a reward, Isla filled his glass again.

He unbuttoned his shirt, revealing a tank top. He tossed the shirt off, pouring some of the oily Extra Virgin Sauce onto his chest.

Isla asked him to twirl right in front of the camera.

He reached for his fly.

Still swaying, he dropped his pants to his ankles, revealing a pair of green-and-pink plaid boxer shorts. Harcourt fumbled with his tank top, finally pulling it clear of his head. The champagne was obviously beginning to have its intended effect.

"This is very nice!" Isla said, showing him a little more thigh.

He had stripped down to his socks and underwear. He hopped on his right foot while he pulled the left sock off. He whirled it over his head in triumph, then flung it across the room.

"You know, I think he could make it in Vegas," Gigi remarked.

Harcourt started hopping on his left leg, trying to get his right sock off.

"OK, girls," Margaret announced. "Let's get ready to make our move."

We opened the back door of the SUV and started to climb out when a car roared into the parking lot. It was a red Cheetah. "Holy shit!" Gigi said. "Antonio?"

He was out of his car and at the back of ours before we knew what to do.

"Hey there," he said amiably, glancing at our odd setup in the back of the Hummer. "Jessica said I should check up on you guys here. Somebody called her. She seemed kind of freaked out." He laughed. "What a crazy bitch. Anna nearly drowns and all she wants to know is where everybody is sending their kids to preschool." Then he looked at us quizzically and said, "So, what are you doing in the parking lot?" His gaze fell to the screen in the back of the Hummer. The high-resolution LCD showed Isla reclining on the bed in the master bedroom, purring encouragements, while Harcourt hopped around in his underwear trying to dislodge his right sock.

"What the fuck!"

Harcourt managed to free himself from the sock. He twirled it over his head, swiveling his hips to lip-trumpet sounds. Isla clapped her hands and said, "Bravo." Harcourt clutched the bottle of Extra Virgin Sauce with one hand, and with the other flung the sock across the room—or, rather, straight toward the video camera. The screen went dark.

"Shirodhara! Shirodhara!" we heard Isla squeal.

"No time to explain," Margaret said to Antonio. "Let's move in!"

We all ran to the door of the Honeymoon Chalet.

It was locked.

"What the fuck!" Antonio shouted again. *"Get out of the way!"* he yelled, running back to his car. Then he revved up his Cheetah like a jet engine and screeched straight for the door of the Honeymoon Chalet. The rest of us dove into the bushes. With a great, cracking thud, the front door came down, along with a couple of side windows and pieces of the front wall. Broken planks and shattered glass littered the open front of the house. The Cheetah came to a rest in the chalet's capacious living room. Antonio jumped out of his car, clambered over the wreckage, and disappeared into the back of the chalet with the yoga mamas in hot pursuit.

Inside, we found Harcourt sitting on the floor, stark naked. He was nursing what looked like would soon become a huge black eye. Isla had run out of the room and Antonio was standing over Harcourt shaking his fist. *"What the hell is going on here?"* Antonio was screaming.

Harcourt looked up and saw Gigi.

"You?" he said. "What are you doing here?"

"That's right, asshole! It's Uncle Tony. And you're *busted!*"

Susan walked in last of all.

"Susan, it's not what it looks like!" Harcourt said when he saw her.

"I know everything," Susan said firmly. Out of her pocket she pulled her necklace—the necklace with the two shellfish lovers. She tossed it at his feet.

"It's over, Harcourt," she said.

"OK, kids," Margaret said, looking at Susan and Harcourt. "No more talking. Let's let the lawyers handle it from here on in."

Everyone was shaking, except Margaret, who preserved her courtroom calm.

"Did we get what we needed?" Gigi asked her anxiously.

"Oh yeah, we did just fine. I think this counts as *in flagrante*." She pulled the sock off the nannycam and panned it across the room, lingering on the naked Harcourt before throwing him a business card. "Have your lawyer call me, when he gets a chance," she said. "We've got some things to discuss."

Behind her, Susan nodded.

I made my way out of the bedroom and found Isla sitting quietly in front of the wrecked Cheetah.

"Antonio did this for me." She was crying softly.

"Isla, maybe—" I sat down beside her and put my arm around her.

"No," she shook her head. "I have been such an idiot." She got up and walked into the garden by herself.

Antonio came and sat down beside me. He seemed to have regained his calm. We sat in silence for a few moments. In the distance I could hear a siren.

"So," I finally said. "Why did you buy a Cheetah?"

He gave me a strange look. "Didn't Richie tell you? It was the ads. I fell for the ads. *Stop the noise . . . Lose the baggage!*"

I swelled with professional pride. That was my idea! I could move cars out of showrooms with six little words, I had a career that would give me independence, a job that paid . . . that paid *nothing*. Robin told me they weren't going to use my campaign idea. That it was "too clever" for them. This was plagiarism! And they never paid me!

"Yeah," Antonio added dryly. "I especially like the bit where the guy zooms off in his Cheetah and leaves the dirty laundry behind."

"But that was *my* idea," I shouted. "They *stole* it from me!"

"To tell the truth," Antonio said wearily, "I wish you'd kept your idea to yourself. I wish I never bought that stupid car. I wish . . ."

Our eyes fell on the Cheetah.

"You know she loves you more than anything," I said.

He said nothing for a long while. "I need a new car," he finally said.

Just then, the police pulled up in the company of Jessica and the Spa Lady. We had a lot of explaining to do.

"It's my car. I did it," Antonio said casually.

"All right, buddy, stand up slowly," the first policeman said.

"She made me do it," Antonio added.

"Tell me something I haven't heard before," the second cop replied.

They snapped cuffs on him, then took him to the squad car.

One of the cops took out a notepad and tried to piece together the story.

The police were as gentle as kittens compared to the Spa Lady. She was beside herself. She could only repeat, hysterically, "*Never again!* You are all on *the blacklist!*"

And later Jessica made the Spa Lady seem a beacon of sanity.

"How could you all *do* this? Cameron will *never* get into Metropolitan now!"

23

Ashtanga yoga has completely changed me. . . . It
makes all the other bullshit dissipate. Who I am has
emerged and everything else has gone by the wayside.

—GWYNETH PALTROW

Isla left for Lanzarote that fall. "I need to go someplace where
everything is dead," she explained. So she sold her loft out from
under Antonio's art collection, packed up her daughter, and
moved to the island where her mother had raised her thirty years
before. Across six time zones, I asked her about Antonio. "He
calls sometimes," she said, trying to sound unconcerned. For a
moment I heard only static, and I thought the line was down.
Then her voice came on again, as fragile as glass. "Azula does not
know her father."

On a brisk November afternoon, Gigi and I paid a visit to Extra

Virgin and spoke to the man behind the terra-cotta tasting bar. Antonio no longer lived in New York, we learned. He was taking the Extra Virgin concept national. The restaurant had bombed in the Village; but the business lunch crowd loved the Mediterranean food, just as Margaret had predicted so long ago, and seniors flocked to the "oily bird specials." "He's in Florida now," the barman said, offering to put us in touch.

"Damn, I miss Isla," Gigi said.

"She'll be back," I promised.

Gigi stuck to juice now—or the Detoxifying Rainforest Blend from Le Refuge, whenever she could get it. At first I figured that maybe it was something about watching Harcourt—the man who, in the end, was not the father of her child—drink himself into a pathetic nudity that had flipped the taps off in her mind. But there was more to it than that.

"We had the Big Talk, me and my Milton," she said one day after yoga.

"And?"

"We're going for number two!"

I was thrilled. With any luck, Gigi was going to be our first two-timer!

She grabbed my arm. "What about you? C'mon, I've seen the way Richie's been pawing you! It's a gross violation of public decency!"

It was true. Ever since that crazy day on Long Island, my marriage had experienced an erotic renaissance. To my astonishment, Richard even took a liking to the ginger-kiwi body oil I snatched at Le Refuge. But we hadn't had the Big Talk yet.

Margaret had developed an unexpected taste for Gaia's style of yoga. Every week or so that winter, I'd meet her under the mesmerizing ceiling fan in Gaia's studio, and she'd give me a hasty update on developments in the Fielding case. "I can't breach client confidentiality," she apologized. But in between the lines, I glimpsed a vast landscape of litigation, involving many branches of the Fielding family and their hidden assets, the owners of Le Refuge, several insurance companies, and the Metropolitan preschool, whose headmistress was keen to contain any damage to its reputation from the activities of one of its (formerly) distinguished board members. Just about everyone had an interest in making sure that the contents of a certain digital video file never made it into the public realm.

"You wouldn't believe how hard it is to get these Fieldings to agree on anything," Margaret told me. "But then when I wave the DVD in their faces, they suddenly become very cooperative."

As the winter wore on, it became clear that Susan was on her way to becoming an extraordinarily wealthy woman. "We're taking them to the cleaners!" Margaret confided. For starters, Susan took possession of the Fielding Manor in the Hamptons, where she and Honor now lived year-round. "I've always been a country girl at heart," Susan explained.

When Susan came into town, I'd often find her giggling with Margaret at the back of Gaia's studio. One day I heard them talking about Le Refuge.

"The owners were giving us grief over the damages," Margaret said, answering my curious stare.

"So I said, 'How about if I buy it?'" Susan laughed. "'The

whole spa.'" There was a new, lively edge in her voice. She seemed a little harder, more practical than the vitamin popper I'd met so long before. "Everybody still thinks she's woo-woo," as Gigi put it. "But inside she's as tough as a nut. Who would have known?"

"Now all we have to do is to make our peace with Metropolitan," Susan added.

I looked at Margaret quizzically.

"Let's just say that the school there has to address certain management concerns we have."

"I'm sorry we can't tell you everything yet," Susan said. "It will all make sense at the right time. Everything happens for a reason."

One of the first words that Anna learned was "mine." She let me know that the teddy bear was "mine," the coffee table was "mine," the streetlamp was "mine"—in fact, the whole neighborhood was "mine." Then one day she scrambled up my lap, wrapped her little arms around my neck, and said, "mine." And I wanted to give her the world.

I thought of Anna's second year of life as the Great Baby Chase. She graduated quickly from toddling to scurrying, and from scurrying to flat-out speed sprints. She never stayed in one place for very long; and, therefore, neither did I. "Hey, it seems like a great way to combine child care with working out," Richard said breathlessly one day. Then he turned around and revealed to me his idea for child leashes. "Think about it," he said. "Why use leashes only on dogs? If we designed one for toddlers, it would be so much more efficient!"

"I have a better idea," I snapped back. "How about husband muzzles?"

He laughed.

The most amazing development that year, as it turned out, was not the sudden heat in our marriage bed; it was that Richard had begun to take on an appreciable amount of child care. "It's Daddy's turn," he liked to say whenever I reached for Anna and she ran to him instead. As Anna learned to speak and roam the world, I realized, Richard found it much easier to be a father.

Richard's newfound helpfulness did not arrive a moment too soon. After I learned about the unauthorized expropriation of my campaign idea for the Cheetah, I called the mother of the other Anna, the one who worked at Amalgamated Motors, and explained the situation to her.

"Sounds pretty vile," she agreed. She asked me to show her my original proposal and dated cover letter.

Within weeks, the agency paid me a hefty settlement. Even better, they offered me an ironclad consulting contract. "We'd like you to spearhead a campaign for Amalgamated's new supersized SUV targeted to security-conscious soccer moms," the company president said.

"I have a job?" I blurted. "What about Robin? Isn't Amalgamated her client?"

"Robin? We fired her. Anyway, I hear she's decided to have a baby."

*   *   *

I knew Isla was coming back when I saw her doing the Warrior One pose on the cover of *Vogue,* baby Azula at her feet. "Isla: Model Mom" ran the title. Motherhood was all the rage these days, and with the help of some savvy marketing, Isla had positioned herself brilliantly as the sultriest super-mommy of the fashion world. I stared at the cover for a long time, trying to penetrate the mystery that lay behind her luminous, moody eyes.

On a beautiful day in June, she landed at JFK, with Azula toddling along at her side in a matching embroidered caftan. For the first time, her face showed the faint trace of weather lines. In a strange way, it only made her more beautiful. We bundled her into the car and headed east along the highway. "I am *so* looking forward to this," Richard said as we motored toward the far end of Long Island. "Who ever heard of a yoga wedding?"

24

Yoga is who you are.
It is your natural state.

—SHARON GANNON AND DAVID LIFE, *JIVAMUKTI YOGA*

"Let us welcome the sun, whose glorious rays bless us with warmth and light," Susan begins.

The yoga mamas (and papas) arrange themselves comfortably in the yoga studio of the Shirodhara Spa—located on the beautiful grounds of what used to be Le Refuge. The gardens outside are bursting with flowers. Apricot, peach, and plum trees swell with ripening fruit, and the air is fragrant with the scent of wild jasmine. The spa is dubbed "A Family Wellness Center" now, and it offers a full range of pre- and postnatal treatments, a special "Daddy Does It" yoga program, and even transcendental meditation for toddlers. The guest rooms have been completely baby proofed and retrofitted with dream catchers, special mountain-goat-hair carpets, and cruelty-free goose-feather mattresses.

"We are gathered here today in the spirit of peace and wholeness," Susan continues. As she performs the Sun Salutation in her flowing white robe, the new owner of the spa is a picture of yogic contentment.

Behind her, two-year-old Honor practices the Downward Dog. Anna sprints up to her side. She tries doing something like a Downward Dog, but falls down and rolls on her back. *Ah, yes, the Flat on Your Back pose,* I think.

Gigi looks serene, standing next to Milton and Charles. She is cradling her newborn, Isabelle, who starts demanding milk with a lusty cry. "My Isabelle, she's just like her mama," Gigi says. "She's got an attitude!" She turns and says to the rest of us, "Come on, you yoga bitches, get cracking! We need more yoga babies!" Milton preens with delight. On the way in, he offers Richard a cigar. Then, as an afterthought, he asks if I want one too.

"How can you be *sure* you'll love the second one as much as the first?" I ask Gigi. Richard and I just started trying for number two.

"Remember the day Anna was born?" she says. "You're screaming and cursing, and then she comes out all perfect, with all her fingers and toes, and you wonder how you could ever love anything else as much. But then the second one comes and she's just as perfect, and she's got all her little fingers and toes, and you just can't imagine life without her."

"Assume Warrior One," Susan commands.

Isla raises her chin high and stretches her fabulously long arms toward the sky. She is hard like mahogany. Her revived modeling career is going extraordinarily well. But you can see in her face that she's not expecting to get any help.

"Assume the Pathway of Love."

This is Susan's innovation. We fall into two lines and extend our arms over the middle, forming an aisle with the arc of welcoming limbs. Behind us, our toddlers wave their arms in all directions.

"Let us welcome the two initiates as they form their eternal bond of wholeness."

The bride is all white silk, interrupted only with a swipe of red lipstick and the shock of stylishly coiffed red hair. She is petite as always, and more beautiful than I have ever known her to be. The groom, too, has tamed his unruly locks. But he's still a little goofy, in a fetching way. On him, the white robe looks like a beginner karate outfit. Behind them the little boy wobbles around in his junior yogi garb.

"Do you, Margaret, accept Jonathan as your eternal lover on the ancient pathway of bliss?" Susan intones.

"*I do,*" says Margaret.

"And do you, Jonathan . . ."

Technically speaking, it isn't a wedding. They've already submitted to a civil ceremony. In fact, together with their lawyers, they've spent most of the previous year hammering out a 100-page document detailing their rights and responsibilities as marriage partners. "So it's the *celebration* of a wedding, legally speaking," as Margaret said to me on the phone. "But it means everything to us."

"*Namaste,*" we chant after they exchange vows.

They kiss with all the passion of two lovers entwined in the whipping cream section, and we shower them with rose petals and organic rice. The children take this as the signal to run rampant. The yoga "wedding" dissolves into laughter and hugs.

As Anna races gleefully around the studio, her footsteps fall like taps upon my heart. I see her through a richly hued cloud of joy and apprehension. I try to picture her in school, scurrying about in her little uniform, negotiating with teachers, bullies, and friends, accumulating new experiences and an identity of her own. The words from the headmistress are still singing in my ear. "Susan has . . . made us aware of your . . . circumstances. And we understand Anna learned to walk *and swim* at the age of eleven months. I want you to know that a full scholarship at Metropolitan is yours for the asking."

I have always encouraged Anna to be a "big girl"; I have worked every hour for nearly a thousand days and nights to make her one, and I have told her many times that she already *is* one. Now it is all coming true before my eyes. She is not yet three, but she has feelings of her own and a handful of words with which to describe them. In my heart I know that I will soon have to let her begin her own journey. "I raised you to be free," I hear my mother's voice in the back of my mind. I tell myself that my daughter is ready for whatever Metropolitan can throw at her. I wonder if I am.

She runs up and wraps herself around my legs.

"Mommy, what is yoga?"

I have to smile.

"Yoga is who we are."

A piece of my soul, a piece I hadn't even known was missing, snaps into place.

And her name is Anna. Definitely Anna.

I couldn't imagine it any other way.

Katherine Stewart is a freelance journalist and writer. She has contributed to *Marie Claire*, *Rolling Stone*, *Elle*, *Fit Pregnancy*, *Conde Nast Traveler* and the *Village Voice* among others. She lives in SoHo with her husband and their daughter. Visit her website at www.katherinestewart.net